THE ALPHABETICAL HOOKUP LIST

K → Q

Phoebe McPhee

POCKET BOOKS
New York   London   Toronto   Sydney   Singapore

This book is a work of fiction. Names, characters, places, and incidents are products of the author's imagination or are used fictitiously. Any resemblance to actual events or locales or persons, living or dead, is entirely coincidental.

An *Original* Publication of MTV Books/Pocket Books

POCKET BOOKS, a division of Simon & Schuster Inc.
1230 Avenue of the Americas, New York, NY 10020

Produced by 17th Street Productions,
an Alloy, Inc. company
151 West 26th Street
New York, NY 10001

MTV Music Television and all related titles, logos, and characters are trademarks of MTV Networks, a division of Viacom International Inc.

ISBN: 0-7434-4843-X
ISBN: 978-0-7434-4843-7

First MTV Books/Pocket Books trade paperback printing August 2002

10 9 8 7 6 5 4 3 2 1

Cover design by Amy Beadle
Printed in the U.S.A.

For information regarding special discounts for bulk purchases, please contact Simon & Schuster Special Sales at 1-800-456-6798 or business@simonandschuster.com

"When in doubt, just cut out."

That had been Ali Sheppard's all-time favorite personal motto in high school. But Ali was in college now, and while class attendance wasn't exactly optional, it wasn't totally mandatory, either. It was *college*. They were *adults*. She had a busy schedule. Nobody was really expected to go to every single class—especially the early morning ones.

Ali pulled her comforter over her head to block out the sun that streamed through the window. College wasn't as exciting as she had thought it would be. The classes managed to sound a lot more riveting in the Pollard University catalog than they did when you were sitting in your hard orange chair watching the professor's mouth move and looking through your tampon case to see if you had remembered to put some Excedrin in there—because Excedrin was the headache medicine, and college gave you one big headache. She just wasn't one of those people who liked to do the same things day after day after day. Except watch *General Hospital* in the Maize Hall lounge. That she *had* to do every day. She was totally addicted. It was too bad that it conflicted with Introduction to Feminist Thought, but what could you do? Priorities were priorities

Ali pushed her dyed black hair away from her face and looked at her fake-diamond-rimmed TechnoMarine watch. It was two o'clock. She got out of bed, put on her fuzzy white polar bear slippers, and straightened the flannel sushi pajamas that had twisted around her body while she slept. That was the other annoying thing about college—you really couldn't sleep in the nude.

She padded along the hall and down the stairs. Aside from the pounding bass line of some techno song coming through the ceiling, the dorm was eerily silent. Did everyone else actually go to class? And if so, how did they stay awake through all the lectures? Maybe the rest of the frosh had been turned on to some powerful upper that Ali had yet to hear about.

Mental note—stock up on No-Doz ASAP.

Ali walked out of Maize Hall into the glaring Georgia sunshine and headed along the green to the mail building. The semicute mail guy behind the counter smiled as she approached. He was wearing a short-sleeved plaid shirt and thin-wale cords, walking that fine line between geeky chic and just plain geeky.

"Do you have anything for Alison Sheppard, Maize, room 213?" she asked.

"One moment, ma'am," mail guy said.

Ali wrinkled her forehead as he disappeared into the

bowels of the mailroom. Had he really called her *ma'am?* Who called anyone *ma'am?*

He returned moments later, smoothed down a cowlicky piece of hair on the side of his head, and handed her a letter. It was from her father. Boring.

"Was there a fire in your room or something?" the mail guy asked, looking her up and down.

"Yeah, actually," Ali said, stifling a yawn. "My next-door neighbor set my roommate Jodi's bed on fire while making hot buttered rum on an electric hot plate. It wasn't pretty. She has narcolepsy."

"Your roommate?" the mail guy asked, his eyebrows shooting up.

"Nope. My neighbor," Ali answered. "But that was a couple of days ago. How did you know?"

"I didn't. I thought . . . well, I figured there was some kind of an emergency and you had to run out in your jammies," he explained with a shrug. "I didn't really think there was a *fire.*"

Ali looked down at her pajamas. Whoops. She'd sort of spaced on the fact that she wasn't dressed. "Actually, I'm starting a new trend," Ali said. "It's called Campus Chic."

"I like it," the mail guy said, smiling.

"Thanks, dude," Ali said, smiling back.

Nothing like early morning flirtation . . . even if it *was* two o'clock in the afternoon and the guy had just called you ma'am.

Ali looked down at the letter from her father. She didn't really want to open the envelope, but she did it, anyway. Call it morbid curiosity. She just *had* to find out what he wanted to scold her for this time.

Ali unfolded the letter handwritten in her father's slanty script—script she had forged perfectly so many times, she could do it with her eyes closed—and a check floated to the ground.

A check? Why had her father sent her a check? It was *so* not him. She bent down and picked it up.

"What'd you get?" the mail guy said.

"None of your bus—"

Before Ali could finish the sentence, he grabbed the check out of her hand.

"Hey! It's a federal offense to read someone else's mail," Ali said.

"Actually, I believe it's a federal offense to *open* someone else's mail. Reading it is just rude," the mail guy said with a smirk. He held up the check and his face went slack. "Whoa."

"Dude, what do you mean by whoa?" Ali asked.

"Looks like Little Miss Fuzzy Slippers is actually Little Miss Rolling In It," he answered, sounding impressed.

"Ha ha, very funny," Ali said. She knew the check in his hands couldn't be for more than ten bucks. Her father wasn't capable of writing more than one zero. "My name isn't Little Miss anything."

"I know," he said, eyeing the check. "It's Alison Millicent Sheppard. And my name's Carl," he added.

"Really? I thought it was Newman," Ali said, smirking.

"Who?"

"Newman. You know, from *Seinfeld?* The fat—"

Ali stopped. Why was she giving the mail guy a hard time? He was actually reasonably cute and nice, and he hadn't even made fun of her middle name.[1] It was too bad his name was Carl and she had already passed *C* on the Alphabetical Hookup List. If she were on *C*, she'd kiss him right now to make up for the Newman comment.

The Alphabetical Hookup List was this crazy thing Ali and her roommates, Jodi and Celeste, were doing. A kind of contest. Basically they each had to kiss one guy for each letter of the alphabet, in order—hence the title of the game. And after a few missteps—kissing a bunch of girls during a temporary bout of lesbianism, making out with a chimp while volunteering at an animal shelter—Ali had gotten herself all the way up to the letter *K* by kissing real, live Homo sapiens of the straight male variety. She was totally going to win.

"It's too bad Carl begins with *C*," Ali said.

"Huh?" Carl said, looking at her like she was crazy. "Actually, it doesn't. It begins with *K*."

Ali smiled. This was turning out to be a profitable trip to the post office, "whoa"-worthy check or no.

"Okay, *Karl*," she said. "How about this? I'll kiss you if you agree to hand over that check right now."

Without a second's pause, Karl handed over the check. Ali snatched it and looked at the amount. Her stomach hit the linoleum. *Six thousand dollars.*

Was this a joke? She looked away, then back at the check.

☐☐☐☐☐☐☐☐☐☐☐☐☐☐☐☐☐☐☐☐☐☐☐☐☐☐☐

1 From Ali's great-grandmother.

Six thousand dollars.

"Six thousand dollars," Ali said, more to herself than Karl. "Six thousand dollars."

Her mouth went dry and she started to walk toward the door in complete shock. Six thousand dollars. All those zeros. Her father had actually written three zeros after a number. Five if you counted those two after the decimal point. . . .

"Aren't you forgetting something, Alison Millicent?" Karl asked. "My kiss?"

Ali turned around, walked over to him, grabbed his shirt front, and pulled him halfway across the counter. "Six," she said, and kissed him. "Thousand," she said, and kissed him again. "Dollars," she said, and kissed him one more time. *"Six thousand dollars!"* she shouted at the top of her lungs.

Then she ran out of the small mail building as fast as her polar bear slippers would take her.

Why the hell had her father sent her six thousand dollars? Had he had a breakdown? A lobotomy? Then she remembered the letter. Ali plunked herself down on the grass in the quad and began reading the note from her wonderful, generous, extremely cool father.

Dear Alison,

I know this will come as a surprise to you, but I have gotten a job as a consultant on an offshore oil rig in the Black Sea, and I will have no access to postal service for the next six months . . .

"Huh?" Ali said out loud. Her father's life was so weird. But at the moment, she couldn't knock him. He'd just sent her an extremely generous gift.

> . . . so I am entrusting you with the enclosed check. As you know, I have an agreement with the bursar to pay your tuition in installments throughout the year, and now this responsibility must fall upon your shoulders.

Gimme a break, Ali thought, her smile quickly fading.

I hope I can trust you to use this check to cover your tuition and living expenses for the remainder of the year. . . .

The whole rest of the letter was just one giant lecture about how she had to be responsible and blah blah blah. Of course she was responsible. What was the big deal, anyway?

She jumped up, ran back to Maize Hall, and got dressed. Then she headed for the ATM at the student center to deposit the check. A few beeps and bleeps and she watched her projected balance change from $49.33 to $6049.33.

Okay, now there were just three things she had to do:

Buy a camera to take a picture of the ATM screen so she could always remember what her bank account looked like with that much money in it.

Write *Karl* next to *K* in her official Alphabetical Hookup List notebook.

Take her roommates out to dinner at an expensive restaurant to celebrate how adult and responsible she was. After all, an expensive meal with friends was a very adult thing to do, right?

2

Jodi Stein dragged herself toward Maize Hall in the middle of the afternoon, hoping that no one would be in the triple. Normally she loved to come home to Celeste and Ali and dish about her day, but right now all she could think about was sneaking a nap on one of their beds. Ever since lazy-eyed, narcoleptic K.J. Martin had burned her bed to a gnarled, angry twist of metal that looked like something out of a Grimms' fairytale, Jodi had been sleeping on a cot. A cot that was just about as comfortable as the cement basement floor back home.

All day, Jodi had been falling asleep in the most inappropriate places—biology class, art history class, and, worst of all, the bleachers during track practice. Coach Calhoun had just sent her home with a very public stern warning. Jodi cringed every time she thought about it. She wasn't used to getting public stern warnings.

As the elevator door opened on the second floor of Maize Hall, Jodi pulled the rubber band from her ponytail and let her thick, sandy brown hair tumble toward her shoulders. Her mouth agape in a huge yawn, she came around the corner. Her heart leapt with joy. There, standing in front of room 213, were two Pollard University custodial-type guys along with lazy-eyed, narcoleptic K.J. Martin herself. The custodians were toting a brand new mattress.

"Oh, yes!" Jodi exclaimed. She rushed past them into her room and saw a perfect bed frame standing where her old, charred one used to be.

"You should be glad I torched your bed," lazy-eyed, narcoleptic K.J. Martin said, crossing her flabby arms as she followed the custodians into the room. "That mattress is better than your old one."

"Thank you, thank you, thank you!" Jodi said to the custodians, jumping up and down in her green and white Pollard U. shorts like a cheerleader on speed.

"I guess you're glad to see us," the younger, less pudgy of the two guys said with a half smile as they slapped the mattress onto the bed.

"Are you kidding? I could kiss you!" Jodi said.

Actually . . .

The last guy she had kissed for the Alphabetical Hookup List was Dirk, the delivery guy who had brought her all her stuff from home. Could she be so lucky as to have found another delivery guy to kiss? Maybe he was an Evan or an Eli or an Ethan. . . .

"What's your name?" Jodi asked, her green eyes narrowing flirtatiously.

"Rick," he replied. "This is Emmit," he added, pointing his thumb over his shoulder.

Jodi looked at the other custodian. He gave her a gap-toothed grin and belched. Jodi winced. She was psyched about the bed and desperate for an *E*, but she did have *some* standards.

"Well, thanks again, guys," Jodi said, ushering them out. Then she turned and flopped onto her new bed. She felt like she was melting into the mattress. "Ahhhhhh!" she moaned, crooking her arms behind her head.

"Come on," K.J. said, rolling her eyes. The right one came back to focus on Jodi, but the left one stayed focused on the wall. "The cot couldn't have been that bad."

"Please. I have permanently bruised vertebrae," Jodi replied. She pulled off her gold rings and placed them on the dresser behind her, then did the same with her gold "Jodi" nameplate necklace. Jodi could never wear jewelry while she slept, unless she was drunk. "Why couldn't you burn your own bed?"

"Who do you think I am, Farrah Fawcett?" K.J. retorted.

"Huh?" Jodi asked. Was it lack of sleep, or did K.J. just not make any sense whatsoever?

"You know, Farrah Fawcett? She starred in a movie called *The Burning Bed*. Oh, never mind. Anyway, I practically burn up the bed every time I get it onnnnn," K.J. said. "Cuz I'm so hot." She touched her finger to her tongue, then to her ass, and made a pathetic little sizzling sound.

"Eeew," Jodi said. The idea of lazy-eyed, narcoleptic

K.J. Martin getting it on was the last thing she wanted to think about. The girl was hygiene-challenged. Jodi still couldn't believe that Kappa Kappa Gamma had given K.J. a bid and completely passed Jodi over. So what if she'd wiped her barf in the sorority president's hair? People made mistakes.

"Well, I'd better get to class," lazy-eyed, narcoleptic K.J. Martin said. "Later for you!"

It was all Jodi could do to keep the groan inside until K.J. left. She turned onto her side, already wondering how she was going to afford new sheets and a comforter for her brand-new bed. It wasn't going to be easy. Ever since her father had cut off her allowance, she'd been working as many shifts at the cafeteria as possible. But the money she made there barely covered the essentials—tampons, lip gloss, and alcohol.

Suddenly, the blinking light on the answering machine caught Jodi's eye, and her heart started to pound. Could it be . . . ?

It's not Zack, she told herself, cringing. *You don't even want it to be Zack.*

Anyway, if it *was* Zack, he was probably just calling to tell her what a delusional freak she was and that he never wanted to see her again. They'd just started to really become friends and now it was over. And she had no one to blame but herself. Moaning, Jodi flipped over onto her stomach and squeezed her eyes shut, trying not to remember the sordid details of the night before last. The bizarre Christian rave, the strobe lights, the little tab of Ecstasy, the way she'd thrown herself at Zack and kissed him.

And he hadn't kissed her back. His lips, in fact, had felt like rigor mortis had set in.

"Jodi, don't," he'd said as he pushed her away. *Jodi, don't. Jodi, don't.* She could still feel the gentle push and see his mouth saying the words. "That's the pill talking. Let's not ruin this," he had said. "We're friends."

Friends. The kiss of death.

"Wait a minute," Jodi said aloud. "This is Zack we're talking about. Weird, crazy-haired Zack. Who cares if he wants to be just friends?"

She pushed herself off the bed, went over to the answering machine and hit the play button.

"Hey . . . Jodi . . . it's Buster—"

"Ugh!"

Jodi pounded the delete button so hard, she almost broke her nail. Just what she needed. A call from her oversexed ex-boyfriend.

She still couldn't really get used to the idea that Buster was her ex. She'd chosen PU mostly so she and Buster could be at the same school. The plan was that they'd go to college together, then get married right after graduation. The plan did *not* include Buster cheating on Jodi with some silicone-boobed slut named Mandi or Bambi or something.

What was *with* these guys, anyway? Buster was running all over campus getting it wherever and from whomever he could—big-boobed Mandi, Jodi's own roommate Celeste (a thought that still made Jodi physically ill)—and meanwhile Zack wouldn't even kiss her while she was on E! Didn't he see a prime opportunity when he was handed one?

Jodi sighed and sat down on her new bed again. Unfortunately, the fact that Zack hadn't taken advantage of the prime opportunity only made her like him more.

3

"My mouth is watering for some non-dining-hall food," Celeste Alexander said. She watched a waiter in a fisherman's hat walk by with a heaped platter of deep-fried clams.

"Tell me about it," Jodi replied. "I haven't been able to eat that stuff since I started serving it. Do you *know* what they put in their omelette surprise?"

"Please don't," Ali said lifting one hand—nails freshly polished psychedelic purple. "The omelette surprise is the only thing I can stomach at the dining hall."

Ali, who usually wore denim jackets and liked her skirts and pants shredded up a little bit in some kind of cross between goth and punk, looked great that evening in a simple short black skirt and scoop neck sweater that was pretty low cut. Her black hair, freed from its usual pigtails, framed her huge black eyes, and her fair skin was luminous.[2]

"Stick with the cereal," Jodi said. "That's my best advice."

□□□□□□□□□□□□□□□□□□□□□□□□□□□□□□□
2 "If one more person says I look like fucking Winona Ryder, I'll kill myself."

Celeste laughed, shaking her curly brown hair back from her shoulders. She took a sip of water and crunched on the ice, enjoying the feel of her elbows resting on an actual table-cloth. She hadn't been to a real restaurant since the semester had started. Back home in New York City, she ate out at restaurants all the time. Her parents never cooked, unless you counted her mother's famous salad sandwiches—not egg salad, not chicken salad, just salad. Or unless you counted hash brownies, something her parents usually made if they were going to one of their hippie reunion potluck dinners.

Anyway, it had been ages since Celeste had eaten in a real restaurant. Of course, the place Ali had chosen for her mysterious celebration wasn't fancy by any means. It was called Tears of a Clam, and it had fishing nets and oars and striped buoys hanging from the ceiling. But there was a flower on the table, and there were chairs that didn't fold. That was something.

"So, what are you guys going to get?" Jodi asked. She looked great, too—just as she had ever since the UPS guys had finally shown up with her clothes. She had on a slim black dress with straps, along with a purple pashmina, and her hair was pulled back from her face.

"I'm not sure," Celeste said. She looked doubtfully at the menu. Truth be told, she wasn't all that crazy about seafood. But Ali was treating them all, so she didn't want to say anything.

Gradually she became aware of male voices behind her. "Darcy's a bitch," one of them was saying.

Celeste shot a quick glance over her shoulder. Three guys

sat at the table behind theirs. She guessed they were all about her age, maybe a few years older. Two of them wore baseball caps. They were all clean-cut, all-American Aber-crombie types.

"I think Darcy's hot," the one in the yellow baseball cap replied. "You should do her. She likes you."

Celeste's mouth fell open. *Do* her? Nice.

"I don't even think of her like she's a girl. That's like saying I should do that big clam over there. Or a pencil sharpener," Blue Baseball Cap said.

By now Ali and Jodi were listening, too. Celeste eavesdropped with a sort of morbid interest. What they were saying was offensive, certainly, but at the same time it was sort of fascinating to watch the male species in action. She felt like she was on an African safari, sitting in her Jeep observing three wild tusked warthogs through binoculars from a safe distance.

"Hey, you said it, not me," Yellow Baseball Cap said. "If your dick is small enough to fit in a pencil sharpener, then you should do a pencil sharpener. Actually, you'd probably have extra room in there."

"I think she's hot, too," the boy without the baseball cap put in, speaking up for the first time. "In fact, I already fucked her."

"Huh. It really is disgusting the way guys talk about women," Ali said thoughtfully.

"I don't believe them!" Jodi fumed. "What total oinkers! I'd like to kick their asses."

"I don't know," Celeste said, running her hand under her thick mane of hair.

"Are you kidding?" Ali said. "I'd think you of all people would be offended."

Celeste bit her lip. She knew Ali thought that she was the world's biggest prude, but she was moving away from that, wasn't she? After all, she had lost her virginity to Jodi's ex-boyfriend, Buster. Not that she was proud of it—she definitely wasn't. It had been a huge mistake. But it should have at least stripped her of the prude image.

"Well, we're sort of doing the same thing, aren't we?" Celeste argued. "I mean, if a bunch of guys had the same conversations we've been having over the Alphabetical Hookup List, we'd think they were sexist pigs."

Ali considered this for a moment. They *had* been pretty callous in some of their conversations. They'd even given guys nicknames like Gross Fredo, Andy the Bloated, and Zit-faced Alex.

"True," she said. "The list could qualify us for pigdom."

"Well, hell," Jodi said, lifting her water glass. "Here's to pigdom."

"To pigdom," Celeste and Ali agreed, clinking glasses with Jodi.

Ali sipped and made a face. "Ugh. Water. Dude, we need some wine over here," she said, returning her glass to the table. "Waiter!"

Celeste looked down at her daring-for-her tummy-baring sweater and sighed. She wasn't much of a drinker—in fact, she'd never really been drunk until she'd met Ali and Jodi. And she'd never done drugs either—not even pot. When your parents are total hippie potheads, pretty much the only thing you can do to rebel is be as strait-laced as possible. She wasn't even excelling at pigdom. So far, she'd only gotten through *B* on the Alphabetical Hookup List, and she wished she hadn't even gotten that far. If she hadn't gotten to *B*, that would mean she wouldn't have slept with Buster. And if she hadn't slept with Buster, she would have never hurt Jodi—a person who was turning out to be one of her best friends.

"Well, this is exciting," Jodi said, lifting her menu. "We're used to ordering our dinner with pepperoni and extra cheese."

"Not tonight," Ali said. "Tonight we're celebrating. Lobsters for everyone."

"Um, maybe the lobster *roll*," Celeste said. She couldn't deal with lobster unless it was chopped up in pasta sauce or rolled up in sushi. To her, a whole lobster looked like a cockroach on a plate.

"You know, lobsters always make me think of Buster," Jodi said sadly. "Buster and I always joked about buying a lobster boat together. Before we broke up, I mean." She looked at the tablecloth, sniffling.

Celeste didn't know what to say. Even though Jodi had already broken up with Buster by the time Celeste slept with him, she still felt so guilty about it. She wished she could manage to get through one full night without thinking about it. Of course, she couldn't actually *think* about the encounter itself since she'd been so drunk, she'd forgotten every last detail.

"Maybe Tears of a Clam wasn't such a good idea," Ali said. "Maybe we should have stuck with Denny's."

"No, no, I can handle it," Jodi said. She sat up straight and shook herself. "I am not going to give up lobster just because Buster turned out to be King of the Assholes."

"You said it, sister," Ali said with a quick nod.

Celeste was relieved when the waiter came over and read the specials. Even better, he was the only waiter cute enough to pull off the rain-slicker-and-fisherman's-hat outfit. By the time he got to the end of the list, Celeste, Ali, and Jodi were all exchanging looks of appreciation. They'd definitely scored on the waiter front. Ali made him repeat the specials, just to keep him around.

"So, ladies, what'll it be?" the waiter asked, pen at the ready.

Jodi smiled. You had to love a guy who used the word *ladies.*

"I'll have the lobster platter," she said.

"Ditto that," Ali said. "And popcorn shrimp and fries for the table."

"The lobster roll," Celeste said quickly, handing back her menu.

"And to drink?" the waiter asked.

Ali tapped her finger against her chin in a thoughtful and mature way. "Give us a bottle of your best Chardonnay," she said. She reached for her bag to get her fake ID if necessary, but the waiter simply took their menus and walked away. She liked him already.

A few minutes later, the Chardonnay came and Ali proposed another toast. "To Chardonnay," she said.

"To Chardonnay," Jodi and Celeste chorused, raising their glasses and giggling.

Actually, the Chardonnay reminded Ali that she was really behind in her French class and had put aside tonight to study. Oh, well. *Quel dommage*, or whatever.

"So, Ali," Celeste said, taking a sip of her wine, "what exactly are we celebrating?"

"My father sent me a check for six thousand dollars," Ali said, producing the receipt from the ATM as proof. Celeste and Jodi were really excited—until Ali read them the letter.

"But Ali," Jodi said. "The money isn't yours. You have to pay the bursar with it."

"But isn't it cool?" Ali said. "To have the money all at once like this? You really feel like you could do something with it."

"You can," Celeste said. "You can pay the bursar."

"I will, I will," Ali said. "Hey, what do you think that waiter's name is?"

"Let's make a small exception to our rules," Jodi suggested. "Whoever can get him to kiss her gets to put his name on her list no matter what letter it starts with."

"What if it's a letter we've already done?" Ali asked.

"Then it will count for whatever letter you're up to, no matter what his name is."

"Fine with me," Ali said.

Celeste just sat there quietly. There was no way she was

going to be able to kiss the waiter. She just wasn't as comfortable with kissing random men as her roommates seemed to be.

Jodi signaled to the waiter, and he came over and refreshed their wine glasses.

"Um, what's your name?" Jodi asked. She always had a way of getting right to the point.

"It's Zane. Why?" the waiter asked.

"Oh." Zane. *He's a* Z, Jodi thought, absently picking up her wine glass. Z *like Zack*. . . . Suddenly she found herself wondering what Zack was doing right now.

"No reason," Ali said, taking over. "We were just wondering, if you could kiss any one of us, which one would you choose?"

Jodi almost did a spit take with her Chardonnay.

"Just out of curiosity," Ali added. She leaned forward slightly, giving Zane a clear view of her cleavage. Celeste sank down a few centimeters in her seat, her cheeks the same bright red as the lobster.

The waiter laughed. "Which one of you girls would I kiss?" he asked.

Jodi grabbed her bag and started rummaging through it, pretending to look for something. As competitive as she was, she didn't want the waiter to pick her. She had sort of reserved her *Z* for Zack.

"Well," the waiter said, looking at them one at a time and smiling devilishly. "I guess I would pick . . ."

Ali looked up at him in anticipation.

"Him," the waiter said, pointing at blue-baseball-cap boy at the next table.

Ali's mouth dropped open. Jodi and Celeste burst out laughing.

"Any other questions?" the waiter asked.

"No, that's it," Ali managed.

The waiter left, and Ali put her head in her hands.

"I can't believe you just did that," Jodi said, dropping her purse.

"Oh my God. That was so embarrassing," Celeste added.

Then all three of them burst out laughing again.

"Oh, and guys," Jodi said. "I forgot to tell you something."

"What?" Ali asked.

"We're not just celebrating Ali getting six thousand dollars—"

"And finally being treated like the adult woman that I am," Ali put in.

"Exactly," Jodi said. "We're celebrating something else, too."

"What?" Celeste asked.

Jodi lifted her newly refilled glass of Chardonnay. "To my new bed arriving this afternoon," she said.

"You're kidding!" Celeste said. "That's great!"

Jodi grinned. It *was* great. Things were really starting to come together. She had a new bed, she had her clothes, she was about to rip into her first post-Buster lobster (maybe she'd even picture his face on it as she tore its legs off). And she was out to dinner with her two best friends. Jodi Stein was definitely moving on with her life.

"To my bed!" she said giddily, holding up her glass.

"To your bed!" Celeste and Ali replied.

4

When they got back to Maize Hall, Celeste produced an extra set of sheets from one of her under-the-bed boxes, and she and Ali helped Jodi make her bed. Jodi sank luxuriously into the nice, clean linens, feeling extremely happy.

"I'm going to wash my face," Celeste said, grabbing her plastic basket of bathroom stuff.

"I'm going to sleep," Ali said, managing to kick off her shoes before she pulled her blanket over her head.

Jodi crawled out of bed and slipped out of her dress, then put on her favorite pair of silky Victoria's Secret pajamas—a pair that used to be reserved for special Buster nights only.

She sighed contentedly and climbed back into bed. She was going to start treating herself right. She really was going to get over Buster. And she really loved her friends. And as for Zack? Well, when she really thought about it, he probably wasn't right for her. She had just been on the rebound from Buster, and Zack had been there for her, and that was all. Zack was just too serious and philosophical and always wanted to have these heavy conversations. Jodi liked to have fun. All of his favorite movies were by Ingmar Bergman.³ Her favorite movie was *Legally Blonde*.

She *should* just be friends with Zack. Who knew what great guy was waiting out there for her? He could be right around the corner.

Celeste came back into the room and switched off the light before getting into bed. "Night," she said.

"Night," Jodi replied.

All that came from Ali was the sound of heavy breathing.

Jodi closed her eyes and thought of all the random guys she'd kissed for the Alphabetical Hookup List—some of whom hadn't counted because she'd gone out of order. But she'd really had fun with the game. Even kissing Zit-faced Alex hadn't been that bad. As she began to fall asleep in total comfort, she promised herself that she wouldn't even *think* about finding a boyfriend until she had completed the AHUL.

The phone rang and Ali answered it, half asleep. Celeste put her comforter over her head, indicating that she wasn't there.

"Jodi, it's for you. It's that dude Zack." Ali yawned.

Speak of the devil. Or think of the devil, to be more accurate. Jodi pushed herself out of bed and took the cordless from Ali.

"Hello?" she said tentatively, sitting down on her bed again.

□□□□□□□□□□□□□□□□□□□□□□□□□□□□□

3 She pretended she had seen them.

"Hey." His voice gave her tingles—a bad sign. "I was wondering if you wanted to get together for coffee tomorrow."

Jodi bit her lip. "Uh . . . sure."

"How about ten o'clock at the Blue Sky?" he asked.

"Okay," Jodi said. "I'll see you then." She clicked off the phone and dropped it back on its base.

"What did he want?" Celeste asked.

"He wants to have coffee in the morning," Jodi said.

She got back into bed and was shocked to find herself smiling from ear to ear. How could it be that Zack of the weird hair actually had this effect on her? She'd just decided that friendship was fine! But if he wanted to meet her for coffee, then . . . well, maybe he'd changed his mind about the friends thing. And if that was the case . . .

Okay, so what if he was deep and philosophical? Maybe it was time for Jodi to try to become a deeper person. They had philosophy classes at PU, right?

Making a mental note to check the course catalog in the morning, Jodi drifted happily off to sleep.

5

Jodi got to Blue Sky Coffee fashionably late at ten-fifteen, due to the fact that she had to change outfits a dozen times. God, she loved her college clothes![4] In a short blue skirt, fucking *awesome* knee-high boots, and a sweater with the American flag on the front, she approached Zack's table.

"Hi," she said. "Sorry I'm late."

"Whoa," Zack said.

Jodi smiled, anticipating a compliment.

"Aren't you patriotic," he said.

Jodi kept smiling, but she wasn't sure what to make of his comment. Was he insulting her?

"It's just a sweater," she said.

"Oh, I know it's just a sweater," Zack said. "I mean . . . I know it's not *actually* the American flag."

This was weird. They were sort of off on the wrong foot. Then again, the last time she saw him, she'd been high on

□□□□□□□□□□□□□□□□□□□□□□□□□□□□□□□□□

4 Next to shopping for what you are going to wear to your wedding, there is nothing more exciting than shopping for your first year at college.

Ecstasy and tried to force herself on him. The awkwardness *could* be attributed to that small fact. *We've got to clear the air*, she reminded herself.

"Well, I love America," Jodi said. "I'm proud to wear the flag on my chest."

"If you were a little more versed in global politics and you knew a little more about how America treats the peoples of the rest of the world, you might not be so proud in your Old Navy sweater," Zack said.

Peoples of the rest of the world? Who said *peoples*?

"First of all, this is not Old Navy—it's Ralph Lauren," Jodi said, her skin warming. "And second, what I wear on my chest is my business."

"Yes, but you *know* everyone's going to notice your chest," Zack said. "No matter what's on it." Then he blushed a little.

What? Score! Not that it mattered, she reminded herself—but it was always nice to know when someone admired you.

"I'm just used to you in *Hello Titty* and *Sexaholic and Proud* T-shirts," he added as the tension between them seemed to pass.

"Yeah, I guess that's true," Jodi said. Before UPS Dirk had shown up with her clothes, Jodi's wardrobe had consisted mainly of Pollard University sweatpants and Buster's colorful T-shirt collection. "My clothes finally came," she added.

"Well, God bless America," Zack said.

"Hey, I thought you were buying me coffee," Jodi said.

"What would you like?"

"Cappuccino."

"No one would call you a cheap date," Zack said, standing.

Date. Date! Jodi thought. Zack had used the word *date*. She watched him speaking to the guy behind the counter. He was wearing jeans and a white button-down shirt with the sleeves unevenly rolled up. He ran his hand through his curly brown hair.

He's not cute, she told herself firmly. He's not. He's . . . weird. And . . . grungy. And so not my type.

But what *was* her type these days? Two-timing frat boys like Buster? Not exactly.

Zack returned with her cappuccino.

"I supersized you," he said. "And here's a Sweet'n Low."

"Thanks, but how did you know I like Sweet'n Low?"

"You're a girl, and you're from Long Island," Zack said, smiling.

"Are you implying that I'm a JAP?" Jodi asked, ripping open the tiny pink packet and emptying its heavenly contents.

"Yes, I am," Zack said. "That's not a bad thing, by the way. I happen to love JAPs. I hope to marry one, one day."

Whoa! This was such a revelation that she decided to let the JAP comment go.

"Why's that?" Jodi asked, stirring like there was no tomorrow.

"It was a joke," he said with a half smile. "Although I am Jewish, and being Jewish is important to me. Uh, I think your cancer-causing substance is properly dissolved at this point." He put out his hand and placed it on Jodi's hand, which was still compulsively stirring.

Jodi's cheeks began to burn. Okay, time to set everything straight.

"Look, Zack, there's something I really want to say," she began. "But first I need a sip of coffee." She took a sip and burned her tongue. "Hot."

"Remember that woman who sued McDonald's because her coffee was too hot?" Zack said.

"What? What does that have to do with anything? Zack, I'm trying to tell you something."

"What is it?" he asked.

Jodi took a deep breath. "I just wanted to say I'm sorry."

"It's okay—the sweater's not *that* bad."

"No, not the sweater," Jodi said. "Come on, you know what I mean. The other night. At the Christian rave. With the Ecstasy. I'm really sorry I, uh, you know, kissed you like that. I think it was just, you know, being on the rebound, and taking that drug. I just sort of saw all these crazy little dancing hearts forming a giant heart around your head, and then before I knew what I was doing, I—"

"Dancing hearts?" Zack asked, laughing.

"Come on, I'm trying to be serious," Jodi said.

"Okay," Zack said. "I'm sorry. Please go on."

"I just wanted you to know I think you're right about us *not* being right for each other. We should definitely just be friends."

"I'm glad you agree with me," Zack said, a little too quickly in Jodi's opinion.

Okay, so everything was fine. It was great. It really was better this way.

"So that's all—I just wanted to say I was sorry."

"Don't be sorry," Zack said. "I understand."

That was a weird thing to say. "I understand." It was a teensy bit on the condescending side. Did he mean that he was just so damned attractive and irresistible that he understood why any girl would be forced to throw herself at him?

"Well, good," Jodi said. "Now, what did you want to see *me* about?"

"I just missed you, that's all," Zack said.

"Oh," Jodi said. There was certainly nothing condescending about that. With the light shining through the plate glass window behind him, bathing him in a sort of golden light, Zack looked a lot like Brandon Boyd from Incubus. "Did anyone ever tell you that you look a lot like Brandon Boyd from Incubus?" she asked.

Zack shrugged. "Yeah, I've heard that from people."

"Anyway, I'm so glad we cleared all this up," Jodi said. "As you know, I'm just coming out of a really long relationship with Buster and I really need my freedom right now. You know, just date people, meet different guys—"

Zack interrupted her. "I figured. That's why I don't think we should go out together like that. You need time to get over Dustbuster, or whatever his name is, and frankly, I'm not interested in sleeping around. I'm more in the mood to get serious with one girl, and you and I are just in such emotion-ally different places."

Jodi was completely speechless. She had never had a conversation like this with a guy. Buster had certainly never said things like "emotionally different places."

"You know one of the things I really like about you?" Zack asked.

Jodi was on the edge of her seat. "What?" she asked.

But before he could answer, lazy-eyed, narcoleptic K.J. Martin walked up, hovering over their table like a dirigible.

"Hey, Jodi," she said. "So, how's the new bed? Your ver-tebrae all healed?"

"Yeah. Everything's great, thanks," Jodi said.

You can go away now, she added silently. She wished lazy-eyed, narcoleptic K.J. Martin would just disappear off the face of the earth. She had been about to hear one of the things Zack liked about her!

Lazy-eyed, narcoleptic K.J. Martin got a chair from another table, dragged it noisily over to their table, and sat down.

"Zack, this is laz—" Jodi stopped herself. "This is K.J. K.J. , this is Zack," Jodi said, wearily.

"Oh, I've heard a lot about you, Zack," lazy-eyed, nar-coleptic K.J. Martin said enthusiastically.

"Really?" Zack said, smiling.

Shit, Jodi thought. *Why did lazy-fucking-eyed, narcolep-tic-fucking-K.J. Martin have to say that?* Now Zack would know she had talked about him.

"Jodi, I didn't say this yesterday because I was in a really bad mood, but I want you to know that I am really so sorry for burning up your bed like that. I just don't know how I'm going to make it up to you. I feel like I owe you, like, a million favors."

"That's not necessary," Jodi said. "Definitely not."

"Yes, it is," lazy-eyed, narcoleptic K.J. Martin said. "I'm there for you, Jodi. Any time."

"Oh, well, thanks but, uh, we're kind of in the middle of a conversation," Jodi said.

"That's okay, don't mind me," Lazy-eyed, narcoleptic K.J. Martin said, resting her chin in her hands with her elbows on the table and looking back and forth between Zack and Jodi. "I'll just be here in case you need anything. And I'm really sorry we're not going to be Kappa Kappa Gamma sisters," she added. "But we'll be friends for life, anyway."

This sucked. It was bad enough being rejected by a sorority that by all natural rights she one day should be president of, but that fact that they had actually accepted lazy-eyed, narcoleptic K.J. Martin was almost too much to bear.

Suddenly lazy-eyed, narcoleptic K.J. Martin's big head hit the table. Her arms had given way underneath her chin like a photographer's tripod collapsing. She was sound asleep, snoring peacefully on the table, which was painted to look like the sky—white fluffy clouds against a light blue background. Lying against the sky like that, lazy-eyed narcoleptic K.J. Martin looked even more like a floating blimp.

"She has narcolepsy," Jodi explained, feeling a tiny bit helpless.

"Gotcha. Ah, look at the sleeping angel," Zack said.

"Uh, well, I'd better get to class," Jodi said.

"Yeah, me too."

Still sleeping deeply, lazy-eyed, narcoleptic K.J. Martin changed position, leaning back in the metal café chair. Then she started sliding lower and lower in her seat, until she had slid completely under the table.

"We shouldn't leave her like this," Jodi said.

"You're right," Zack said. "The least we can do is tuck her in."

He took her coat off the back of her chair and spread it out on top of her under the table.

"Well . . . see ya," Jodi said at the door of the café. She hated leaving their conversation right smack in the middle, but she didn't have much choice.

"Yeah," Zack said. "See ya."

Jodi turned and headed for her class, wondering if and when she and Zack would have a chance to continue their chat. And if and when she'd ever find out exactly what it was he liked about her.

6

Celeste sat in her music humanities class listening to Professor McKean drone on about Gregorian chants. Funny how many religions used chanting. . . . When she was a kid, about five or six, her parents had been really into this ashram in Woodstock and would always bring her there on the weekends. Everyone would sit on the floor in the meditation hall and chant Hare Krishna and things like that. She always thought the chanting was a little scary. One time she stood up and, screaming at the top of her lungs, asked, "Mommy, why is Krishna so hairy?" Her parents loved to tell that story.

"Miss Alexander? Miss Alexander?"

Celeste sat up with a start. The teacher had apparently asked her a question and she hadn't even heard it. It was very unlike her to daydream like that.

"I'm sorry, Professor McKean, would you mind repeating the question?" She heard a few people giggling around her.

"No problem," Professor McKean said sarcastically. "In

the year 1345, the composition of the *Poissy Antiphonal* began. Can you tell us what else began—"

"Um, Professor McKean," a voice from the back row called.

"What?" Professor McKean snapped.

"I'm sorry to correct you, but the composition of the *Poissy Antiphonal* actually began in 1335, not 1345."

A girl in Celeste's row hid a laugh behind a cough, and Celeste shot her a smile. She was petite and pretty with light brown hair in braids, and she was wearing a Lesbian Alliance T-shirt.

"Loser," the girl mouthed, shooting McKean a glance and then looking back at Celeste.

"Is that so, Mr. . . ." McKean looked down at his record book.

"Mann. Mr. Mann," the guy in the back row said.

The bell rang and a very annoyed Professor McKean said, "Class dismissed."

Celeste stood up and the Lesbian Alliance girl walked over to her. "Hey," she said. "I'm Eve."

"Celeste," she responded, turning away from Eve for a moment to scan the back row. She didn't want to be rude, but she had to get a glimpse of the guy who had saved her from answering a question she had no idea how to answer. She almost always did all her reading and was prepared, but with the dinner at Tears of a Clam she had sort of blown off her work.

The guy, who at this moment was being treated like a bit

of a celebrity for so gracefully humiliating a teacher, looked older than the other freshmen, Celeste noticed. He really did look like, well, a *man*.

"So, listen, we're having a party tonight at the student center," Eve said, holding out a little slip of pink paper. "You should show."

Celeste's face burned with embarrassment as she looked at the invitation. It was a Lesbian Alliance dance. "Oh! I'm not . . . I mean . . . I don't . . . I wouldn't—"

"I know you're not gay," Eve said sharply, her eyes narrowing angry slits. "God, people are so narrow-minded. Like I'd only invite lesbians. You know what? Forget it!" She grabbed the invite out of Celeste's hand and stalked off before Celeste could even find her tongue.

"Oookay," Celeste said aloud. Some people were just a little too touchy. She gathered her things and headed for the back of the room to catch up with her savior.

"Hey, thanks," she said as she passed him.

He smiled at her and held open the door so she could pass through.

"Actually, I owed you one," he said.

"What do you mean?" Celeste asked.

"Well, you probably didn't even realize this, but a few weeks ago he asked me a really impossible question about the invention of the sitar, and you yelled out the answer. I guess you really know your sitars."

Knowing about sitars was hard to avoid when you had parents like Jib and Carla. "Yeah, I'm kind of a sitar fanatic,"

Celeste cracked. Hey, she was getting pretty good at snappy comebacks!

Mr. Mann laughed, and Celeste blushed. They paused outside the lecture hall and stepped to the wall to let the steady stream of students pass.

"Anyway, thanks again," Celeste said, pushing a wayward curl away from her eyes.

She couldn't help staring at him. Who was this guy? He was sort of cute, in a moppish, Beck-circa-1996 kind of way. But he was too old to be a student. He looked like he was at least twenty-five. She blushed again, remembering that she had just cracked a joke that had made him laugh. She wasn't used to making older men laugh.

"Hey, how did you know the year of that Poissy thing, anyway?" Celeste asked, wondering if he was some kind of music genius or something.

"Um, it was in the reading," he said, with a gently sardonic smile.

"Oh, right," Celeste said, blushing even more and looking down at the tiled floor.

"But don't feel bad. It seems McKean didn't do the reading either. My name is Carter," he said. "Carter Mann."

"I'm Celeste Alexander," she said, suddenly thinking her name sounded awfully formal in a Jane Austen sort of way. "Are you a music major?" she asked as they started to walk down the hall.

"Actually, no. I'm in the school of general studies. But I love music," Carter answered. "Right now I'm taking a break from my business, which is probably one of the crazier things I've ever done, because it was doing so well. I make and distribute concert T-shirts."

"Oh, wow," Celeste said, not so much because of the whole concert T-shirt business thing, but because it had just registered that his name was *Carter*. With a *C*. The next letter she needed. Hallelujah. Praise Hairy Krishna. He was a little old for her, but what the hell? She didn't have to marry the guy. She just had to give him one little kiss. And it was so cute and mature the way he was bragging about what a good businessman he was.

"Yeah, it's great," Carter said, holding open yet another door for her. "I started it from the ground up, but I never finished college, and I always felt kind of guilty about that, so I thought I'd do some self-improving with a little adult education."

The way Celeste blushed, you would think he had said "adult film" instead of "adult education."

"You know, if you tell me your favorite bands, I can get you some T-shirts," Carter said.

Celeste froze. She didn't know what her favorite bands were. She didn't think she had any. She had been to a Barry Manilow concert once on a field trip at camp, but she couldn't say *that*. God, why was she so stupid?

"Uh, the Beatles. John Elton," Celeste said finally.

As soon as she said it, she knew she had meant to say Elton John, which was a stupid answer anyway. Was Elton John even considered to be a band?

"John Elton?" Carter asked, screwing up his forehead a little.

"No, the John Eltons," Celeste said as convincingly as possible. "They're a band I like from New York."

"Huh. I've never heard of them," Carter said. "And I'm not so easily stumped. I'd love to hear their stuff."

"Yeah, you should. They're really great," Celeste said, completely mortified with herself.

"Maybe you could bring me a tape? I mean, if it wouldn't be too much trouble."

She really liked him. He seemed so friendly—especially considering he was a grown-up businessman and she was just a freshman in college. But she was no child, Celeste reminded herself. She was eighteen. And if this nice, interesting, successful guy was interested in talking to her, why should she run away all scared?

She thought of the scene in *Little House on the Prairie* when Laura Ingalls meets Almanzo Wilder for the first time and accidentally calls him Manly instead of Manny. Come to think of it, Laura Ingalls was a lot younger than Almanzo, and she'd ended up marrying him and becoming Laura Ingalls Wilder. But why was she thinking about something so babyish as *Little House on the Prairie* at a time like this? She just hoped she didn't call Carter "Mr. Manly."

"All right, Mr. Mann, I'll bring you a tape," Celeste said.

She turned to leave. "Nice meeting you, Celeste," Carter said.

"Nice meeting you too, Carter," Celeste said. As soon as

she was safely out of earshot she whispered to herself, "Nice meeting you too, Mr. Manly."

When she got a few feet away from the building, she took out her list and, in a bold, confident, and very un-Celeste-like move, she wrote *Carter Mann* next to the letter *C*, as if it were a *fait accompli*. She was going to kiss Carter Mann, and that was that. No matter what impossible task she had to accomplish to do it.

7

Ali was late to French class, as usual. She looked at her watch as she blew through the door and hurriedly took her seat. It was twelve-twenty and class started at twelve. Tiny droplets of black-tinted water flew from her hair, which she'd just finished redying.

"Well, *bonjour*, mademoiselle," Monsieur Schwartz said in his pinched, nasal voice.

That meant "good day," Ali thought. She was almost certain of it. So far, so good.

"*Bonjour*," she said confidently.

"You're early this afternoon," Schwartz said. "We weren't expecting you for another ten or fifteen minutes."

"Sorry," Ali said. "Uh . . . *Excuse moi*." She beamed. She was doing well today.

"Do you want to tell us why you were late today?" Monsieur Schwartz asked. "We'd love to hear what you were doing with your valuable time."

"Ohhhh, *shiiiiiit*," she heard some kid trill under his

breath. Everyone was staring at her. She suddenly felt like she was having some kind of horrible high school flashback moment.

"Really, why were you late?" Monsieur Schwartz repeated, crossing his gangly arms over his pink polo.

"I was in Paris?" Ali tried. "I wanted to practice my French. I just flew in on the red-eye."

Monsieur Schwartz turned a dark shade of red.[5] "Well, Alison, I'd love to hear all about your adventures after class, if you could spare a few moments for me," he said.

Ali lowered her head, wishing she were anywhere but here. Why had she ever thought it would be fun to learn French? It was like a foreign language to her.

Monsieur Schwartz wrote a whole bunch of French on the blackboard. It looked like a song or a poem.

"This is a very challenging piece of French literature," he said. "The translation is difficult. I'm offering it as extra credit. Whoever is the first student to come in with the translation will score points. And you will receive even more points if you can tell me who wrote it."

Monsieur Schwartz began going over the homework from the night before, which Ali hadn't done. As he conjugated and corrected, Ali squinted at the board. The words were blurry because she had gotten up so late, she hadn't had time to put in her contacts. Schwartz's neat script danced around as if the words were animated on a movie screen.

5 *Rouge.*

Wait a minute, Ali thought as she made herself focus. She'd seen that French stuff somewhere before. She knew what it meant.

Maybe she was hung over from the Chardonnay or maybe she was just sick of the boring day-after-day drone of her life in college, but something made her stand up.

Monsieur Schwartz ignored her for as long as possible and then stopped what he was saying. *"Oui?"* he asked.

"I know the translation."

A few people in the class laughed, not even trying to muffle their enjoyment of what was sure to come next.

"Très amusant," Monsieur Schwartz said. "We're all very impressed. Now, if you don't sit down, I'll have you recite your translation to Dean Redding."

Ali focused on the word *Madeleine* on the board. It was Proust. She knew it was Proust. *Remembrance of Things Past.* Sensei, her ex-boyfriend, had gone through a phase where he read passages from the twelve-inch-thick book aloud, first in French and then in English, as part of one of his DJ routines. Ali had never consciously listened to the words, but somehow they must have stuck.

As if she were channeling someone, perhaps Proust himself, Ali recited the translation. The class, and Schwartz, fell silent. It was more of a religious experience than both her Protestant period and her stint with Buddhism. It was a miracle. Definitely an "Ali in Wonderland" moment.

When she was through she sat back down calmly in her chair, exhilarated. "It's by Marcel Proust," she added.

"How did you know that?" Monsieur Schwartz said. His jaw hung open like a giant nutcracker waiting to receive a nut.

"I'm not exactly sure," Ali admitted.

"You must have cheated. An upperclassman must have told you. I give the same assignment every year."

Okay, now Schwartz was actually being insulting.

Everyone was very quiet. The class moved their heads back and forth from Ali to Monsieur Schwartz in perfect precision like spectators at a tennis match.

"Class is over," Monsieur Schwartz said. "Alison, I want to speak to you."

The other students stood and began to file out. You could tell they didn't want to leave; they wanted to witness the throw-down that was about to occur. Ali stayed in her seat, trying to control the fluttery feeling in her stomach. "I demand to know how you knew that," Monsieur Schwartz said.

"I just knew," Ali replied.

"That is not a satisfactory response. You will not receive extra credit for the answer. At this time I must also inform you that you are on the verge of receiving a failing grade."[6]

"That's not fair!" Ali protested.

"I'll tell you what's not fair," Schwartz said. "You've been either late to or absent from every single class for the entire semester. You're obviously a bright girl, and you have a lot of potential. . . ."

□□□□□□□□□□□□□□□□□□□□□□□□□□□□□□□□□

6 Ali was also on the verge of failing Introduction to Feminist Thought, due to the fact that she'd only been there once.

This was where Ali zoned out and the teacher's voice faded and was replaced by that incomprehensible *whomp, whomp, whomp* sound like the grown-ups made in the Peanuts cartoons. How many times had she heard this speech before? About how bright she was and how she had so much potential. That was becoming Ali's least favorite word. *Potential*. Fuck potential.

In her head, Ali did some quick math (another subject she hated). If she flunked French, she could still keep a satisfactory GPA if she aced everything else. But what were the chances of that? It was beginning to sink in that she could actually be in some kind of trouble here. She had been so involved with stuff like volunteering at the Wrinkled Peach and the animal shelter that she really hadn't done a lot of schoolwork. And of course there was the AHUL, which was sort of becoming an obsession. That took up a lot of time.

But Jodi and Celeste were into the AHUL, too. And she didn't see them doing too much studying. Somehow, though, they were doing okay. Why was she the only one having problems?

Schwartz was still gabbing, and Ali was sick of it. She rolled her eyes and walked out of the classroom. Fuck Schwartz. There was nothing French about him. He was from Florida, and he had a German name!

Ali paused in the hallway and took a deep breath. She didn't want to admit it, but Schwartz had made her nervous. Maybe it was time she started taking things more seriously. In fact, maybe it was time she actually opened the course books.

8

As she entered the Allween Library, Jodi inhaled the musty book smell and smiled contentedly. Just being here made her feel more intelligent. More . . . collegiate.

She wondered if Zack was here right now.

"That is not the point," Jodi said under her breath. The point of being here was to get a job. To get the hell out of the dining hall. To never work again in a place where the bathroom signs that had once read *Employees Must Wash Hands Before Returning to Work* had long ago been changed to *Employees Must Not Use Hamburger Rolls to Wipe Asses.*

Yesterday afternoon Jodi had accidentally, coincidentally run into Zack when she was doing her laundry. Okay, she was doing it in *his* dorm's laundry room, but that was only because she had heard a definite rumor that one of the dryers in her dorm's laundry room was eating quarters. It wasn't that she wanted to see him or anything.

But while they were there, transferring their clothes from washer to dryer, he had happened to mention to her that he had gotten a new job shelving books in the cavernous, dimly lit stacks of the library. It sounded lonely and mysterious.

Jodi had made a mental note of this and had then taken one of her sexiest pairs of pink thong panties out of the gentle cycle. She laid them gently out on a towel because they were much too delicate to throw in the dryer. But Zack didn't seem to notice. He just threw his boxer-briefs into the machine, slammed down the lid, and told her that it was great to see her but he "had to jump."[7]

That night, at the dining hall, she had realized what a vastly empty experience her job really was. Sure, she was earning money, but was she really serving society by dusting off old boxes of Tater Tots and making sure the Roach Motels weren't booked to capacity? And if she wasn't furthering humanity, was she at least broadening her own horizons? No!

Zack was smart to work in the library. *He* was sending students on their road to greatness by putting the books they needed in their proper places. All *she* was doing was sending them to the infirmary with nausea and diarrhea.

So here she was at Allween, ready to apply for a new, more worthwhile job. After all, she had come to PU to learn, not to sling hash.

"Um . . . can I help you?" the obvious grad student behind the counter asked.[8] He had shaggy red hair and a shadow of peach fuzz around his mouth. Someone should

☐☐☐☐☐☐☐☐☐☐☐☐☐☐☐☐☐☐☐☐☐☐☐☐☐☐☐☐

7 An annoying thing men say when they have to get going.

8 One can always tell a grad student by the look of disdain he or she gives an obvious undergrad.

have told him that goatees were out everywhere but in the National Hockey League.

"Yes. I was wondering who I could talk to about applying for a job," Jodi said with her best responsible tone.

"You can talk to me," grad-student boy said, pushing himself off his stool.

Oh, goody, Jodi thought.

"Come on back," he said. He looked at the kid on the stool next to him. "Think you can manage to watch the desk while I'm gone?"

The kid lifted his droopy eyes to look out across the deader-than-dead reference room. "I think I can handle it," he said, and returned to his *MAD* magazine.

Jodi followed grad-student boy into a tiny, well-lit office behind the reference counter. He lowered himself into a creaky chair and kicked back, putting his feet up on the desk.

"I'm Hank," he said, crooking his arms behind his head.

"Jodi Stein," she replied, perching on the edge of the cracked vinyl chair across from him.

"Are you familiar with the alphabet?" Hank asked her.

Jodi laughed.

"I'm serious," he said. "How are you with the alphabet?"

"What do you mean?" Jodi asked. Surely this must be a trick question.

"I *mean* do you know your ABCs?" Hank said, speaking very slowly as if she were mentally challenged. He lowered his feet to the floor and leaned forward. "Can you, for instance *alphabetize* something? Say, like, books, for instance."

He sounded as if he were asking her if she could perform neural surgery.

"Of course I can alphabetize books," Jodi said.

"Well, we're screening people more carefully now," Hank said. "I'm afraid I'll have to test you."

He pulled six books from a packed shelf along the wall and slapped them down on the desk.

"Alphabetize these by the authors' last names," he ordered.

Jodi shook her head in disbelief but smiled at the same time, thinking of the Alphabetical Hookup List. She, Celeste, and Ali were *great* at alphabetizing things, especially men.

She arranged the books in their proper order, and Hank seemed very pleased. "Congratulations. You're officially a stack hack, otherwise known as a stacker."

Jodi smiled again. That had been the easiest interview in history.

"So, when can you start?" Hank asked, standing.

"I'm kind of free now," Jodi said, ready to just jump in.

"Great!" Hank said, his eyes bright. "There's a couple of guys working on the fifth floor. They can show you where the newly returned books are."

"Okay," Jodi said, already wondering if Zack was one of those guys.

She started out past the reference counter. "Oh, and Jodi?" Hank said, following her out. "Good luck."

Jodi crinkled her forehead. Why would she need luck? What was so tough about alphabetizing books?

She soon found out why Hank had been treating her like such a freak. Apparently the only people who had applied for jobs at Allween besides her and Zack were Russian and Ukrainian exchange students, all of whom were baffled by the Roman alphabet. Serge and Yevgeny did show her where the books were, but they were full of questions themselves.

"Which one is letter *A* again?" Serge asked, holding up a copy of *Portrait of the Artist* with a completely bemused expression on his face.

"There is no *A* in Joyce," Jodi answered patiently.

"Hey! What are you doing here?" a voice behind her asked.

Jodi smiled, smoothed the front of her pink T-shirt, and turned around.

"Oh, hey," she said to Zack. "I work here now." Then she looked at him with a fake-confused expression before letting her eyes light up with realization. "Oh! That's right! You said you worked here, too."

"Yeah," Zack said, smiling. "This is great!"

He seemed genuinely glad to see her, but maybe that was because she was the only one present who spoke English fluently.

"Hey! Let's go shelve on two," Zack suggested, grabbing her arm and pulling her away from the other guys. "It's going to be so much better working with you than working with the Russian Mafia," he added when they were safely inside the elevator.

Jodi laughed. Damn, she loved Zack's sense of humor.

They hit the second floor and within five minutes of shelving books side by side, they were laughing so hard that studying students all around them were shushing them with annoyed expressions. Jodi couldn't stop smiling. She and Zack just seemed to have good chemistry. Brad Pitt and Jennifer Aniston—move over!

9

Celeste walked into music humanities class the following week and scanned the room, trying to look like she was deciding where to sit. Carter Mann was nowhere to be found. Celeste looked down at her carefully chosen outfit—blue sleeveless J. Crew sweater and almost form-fitting chinos. Had she gone to all that trouble for nothing?

She finally took a seat at the front of the room, then immediately regretted it. From this vantage point, she couldn't see either of the doors without turning around in her seat. What was wrong with her?

"All right, class, I don't feel like lecturing today, so we're going to do something a bit different," Professor McKean said when he walked in. "Pop quiz!"

There was a collective groan. What, was he kidding? This wasn't eighth grade! He handed Celeste a stack of papers.

"Pass these back, please," he said.

Celeste took a page, thanking Hairy Krishna that she'd done the reading this time, then turned to hand the quizzes to the girl behind her. As she did, she caught a glimpse of Carter Mann sitting in the back row. He smiled and lifted his hand in greeting.

Blushing, Celeste faced front again, wishing she had paid more attention to her back when she'd gotten dressed. She should have worn her hair up to show her neck or done something back-attention-grabbing.

Before tucking her planner under her desk, Celeste sneaked a peek at his name next to *C* on her list. She hadn't been able to get Carter out of her mind. She had to at least *try* to kiss him. But how was she going to manage to do that when she couldn't even get up the courage to wave back at him?

When she was done with her quiz, Celeste decided that she would wait for Carter to finish and ask him to have a drink with her. Of course she had never asked anyone to have a drink with her in her life, but if she couldn't at least do that, then she should just drop out of the AHUL contest right now. She absolutely had to get past *B*. Why was she making such a big deal about it anyway? She didn't have to have sex with him; she just had to kiss him.

Celeste gathered her stuff and dropped her quiz on McKean's desk. As she turned to leave, she saw that Carter was getting up as well. She walked out and waited for him in the hallway. Carter came out moments later.

"Hey," he said when he saw her standing against the wall.

"Hey," Celeste said, smiling.

"I got you something."

Celeste couldn't believe what she was hearing. He had

gotten her something. Which meant he had thought about her. Which meant maybe he liked her.

He tossed her a rolled up baseball-style T-shirt.

"It's Linkin Park," he said.

"Oh, thanks, this is great," Celeste said, holding the shirt out in front of her and admiring it. "Linkin Park, I love him."

"Them," Carter corrected.

"Yeah, them, that's what I said," Celeste said quickly.

"I thought you might," Carter said. "All the kids like them."

Oh, great. "Kids"? He wasn't that much older than she was. Was he?

Two girls and a guy burst from the classroom giggling and started talking at the top of their lungs. They stopped right across the hall from Celeste and Carter. The girls were giggling so hard, they were practically convulsing.

"I don't see what the big deal is," the guy said. "I mean, there's really no difference between wearing underwear and not wearing underwear."

"You mean you're not wearing any underwear right now?" the shorter girl choked out between giggles.

"Nope."

More laughter. Celeste really wished these people would go away. It was hard to concentrate on what Carter was saying and the fact that these girls were freshmen, too, and were acting like they were about twelve, made *her* seem younger.

"Celeste, there's something I want you to know," Carter said seriously.

"What?" Celeste asked.

"I'm wearing underwear," Carter said. "I much prefer it that way."

Celeste blushed. "Me too," she said. She wasn't sure if she had told him that she was also wearing underwear or that she preferred him to wear underwear too, but it didn't matter because he laughed.

"Hey, Carter, would you like to have a drink together sometime?" Celeste said. There! She had done it! She liked this new her. This was College Celeste. Sexy, Confident, Chardonnay-drinking Celeste.

It hadn't even been that hard. Soon she and Carter would be sitting in a smoky booth somewhere drinking wine and discussing Linkin Park.[9]

"That's a really nice offer, Celeste. But I'm not really much of a drinker," Carter said.

"Oh." Celeste deflated instantly.

"Well, see you next class," Carter said.

Crushed, Celeste mumbled a good-bye and turned to leave, but he stopped her. "I don't drink that much, but I do enjoy a walk in the park and a spliff every once in a while." He grinned at her. "What about you?"

"Oh, uh . . ." She tried to think of how to answer, considering she'd never smoked pot in her life, but luckily, he spoke first.

"Wait a minute, what am I saying? I can't ask you out yet," Carter said. "I don't even know how old you are."

"How old am I?" Celeste said, racking her brain for a

☐☐☐☐☐☐☐☐☐☐☐☐☐☐☐☐☐☐☐☐☐☐☐☐☐
9 She should probably go buy one of their CDs.

smooth answer. "Well, I'm old enough to get some killer pot. Probably the best you ever had." Oh God. Who was she now, Drug-dealing Celeste?

Carter laughed. "Cool," he said. "So how about tomorrow? Around four?"

"Okay. Why don't we meet in front of my dorm?" Celeste suggested. "Maize Hall?"

"I'll be there," Carter said, putting his hands in the pockets of his baggy, well-worn chinos. "Later."

"Later!" Celeste said.

She turned and allowed herself a little under-her-breath "Yes!" before rushing back to the triple. She could sense that Carter was reluctant to get involved with a freshman, but some of her father's pot would definitely change his mind. Finally, having weird, druggie, overly liberal parents was going to come in handy.

A few minutes later, Celeste slipped through the door of room 213 and grabbed the phone. She dialed her old familiar number in New York and her father answered.

"Hi, Jib," she said.

"Hi, honey," Jib said. "Your mother and I were just talking about you."

"Well, I'm about to make you very proud," Celeste said.

"You've decided to go to medical school?" Jib asked, happily.

"No, I'm not going to be a doctor," Celeste said.

"Not law school," Jib said. "I hate lawyers. I would kill myself if I thought my seed had produced another lawyer in this world."[10]

10 When Celeste was five, her parents cried when she told them that she wanted to take ballet instead of free-style modern dance.

"No, that's not it," Celeste said, not really that thrilled to hear about her father's seed. Although she *was* interested in another kind of seed. "I finally feel like I'm ready to try smoking pot. And you and mom always said you wanted me to come to you for it, so—I'm coming to you."

"Oh, baby, your mother and I are so proud of you!" Jib said. "I just wish we could be there with you. I think you'll find it to be a really mind-opening experience. Wait a minute, let me tell your mother. Carla, our little girl is finally going to get high!"

"Oh, that's wonderful," she heard her mother say.

"Honey, don't cry. Celeste, your mother's crying. This is truly a great day. We really are so proud of you. I'll send you a nice batch of some of our homegrown and some rolling papers. If I get to UPS now, you'll get it by tomorrow morning. I just wish I could be there to show you how to roll your first joint."

"That's okay, Jib. I've watched you and Carla roll so many, I think it'll come pretty naturally," Celeste said.

"You're a chip off the old block," Jib said. "Whoops, I'd better go if I'm going to get this to you by tomorrow."

Celeste clicked off the phone and lay down on her bed. God, her parents were so weird, but that wasn't exactly news.

She just wished Jodi and Ali were here right now so she could tell them all about Carter.

10

"This Dewey Decimal guy was one twisted little fucker," Ali said as she turned down yet another row of musty, dusty books at the Allween Library. Her favorite boots squeaked loudly as she made her way along the shelves, glancing over titles like *Our American Sisters: 1800s to the Present*, and *Slavery and Misogyny*, and wondering who in God's name would ever want to read them. And if they *did* want to read them, how would they ever find them?

Ali had decided to crack down and give this whole "potential" thing a try, but Dewey and his decimals were obviously conspiring against her, as was the whole Pollard University system in general.

Ali's first order of business had been to try to get a grip on the Intro to Feminist Thought class she hadn't attended since day one. Unfortunately, the bookstore had sold out of every last book for the course last week. The chick behind the counter, in fact, had looked at her like she was deranged when she'd asked about it. Not one to give up easily, Ali headed for the library, where she was promptly rebuffed by a guy with a straggly goatee who had actually said, in a very firm voice, "No ID, no entry."

Back to the dorm Ali went, sweating in her black tights and distressed denim mini. She'd torn apart her room looking for her Pollard University ID and finally found it in her orientation packet. So far the only satisfactory moment of her day had been the moment when she'd shoved said ID card in Goatee's face and he'd had to step aside and let her through the hallowed doors of Allween.

So now here she was on the fourth floor, trying to track down a copy of *The Beauty Myth*, which was apparently some kind of feminist propaganda. She was actually kind of psyched to read it—propaganda of any kind was usually pretty fun—but the closest she'd come to the title was *The Big Book of Greek Myths* about twenty minutes ago.

Desperate, Ali looked up and down the row and finally caught a glimpse of a shortish, darkish, dorkyish guy shelving books. Yee-freakin-ha! Someone who actually worked here! This guy had to know what he was doing.

Maybe if she was lucky his name would even start with an *L*. A good kiss was exactly what Ali needed right now to snap her out of her frustrated funk.

"Excuse me," she said, approaching the guy. He simply continued shelving. How rude.

"Um . . . excuse me," Ali said, snapping her fingers close to the guy's face.

He shook his head, startled, and turned his wide-set brown eyes on her. "You talk to me?" he asked.

"Uh, yeah," she said. "Do you know where I can find *The Beauty Myth*?" She looked down at the tiny scrap of paper on which she'd written the book's corresponding numbers. "This whole thing is like Russian to me."

The shelver's face lit up. "You speak Russian?"

"No. Sorry," Ali said, trying not to look too exasperated. "Look, can you help me find this or what?"

"Beauty . . . myth," the guy said carefully. "It starts with *B*?"

He seemed just a little bit too pleased with himself for figuring that one out.

"You know what, forget it," Ali said. She stuffed the paper scrap into her black vinyl bag and scurried away from the stacks. Clearly the fates did not, in fact, want her to realize her full potential. Besides, *General* was starting in less than fifteen minutes.

Back outside in the scorching heat, Ali turned her steps toward Maize Hall, already salivating over the microwave popcorn she always ate when she watched *General*. She was cutting behind the mail building when the sun reflected off a parked car and just about blinded her. Ali stopped to dig in her bag for her sunglasses, but the moment she paused, some guy on Rollerblades slammed into her. Hard.

Ali's bag went flying, spewing her stuff all over the ground.

"Hey!" she shouted unoriginally. The Rollerblader didn't even look back.

"Asshole," Ali said under her breath as she stooped to gather her stuff. She shoved it all back in her bag at random and slipped her sunglasses over her eyes. As she stood again, something bright and pink caught her attention.

On the wall of the mail building was one of those "You are here" maps for lost freshmen, housed under a glass casing. Stuck to the front of it was a hot pink flyer. Ali read the headline. *Double, Triple, Even Quadruple Your Investments!*

Now, *that* was a hell of a lot more interesting than any feminist propaganda. She grabbed the flyer, feeling suddenly psyched. Maybe this was a chance to prove her father wrong about her! She could take the six thousand dollars—well, the five thousand, nine hundred—and quadruple it. Or she could take a smaller portion of it, invest it wisely, and *still* end up with a profit. This was fantastic.

She turned and walked back to Maize to make the call and find her check book. She also had to find Jodi and Celeste. This definitely called for another girls' night out.

11

Ali was on top of the world. She felt so official. So . . . adult. Here she was, in an actual office, wearing actual sensible shoes,[11] handing over a check to an actual investment broker. At least that's what she *assumed* this guy's title was. If her father could see her now.

Okay, so the office itself was tiny and dingy. And it had that overtly clean smell like someone had sprayed Lysol seconds before she came in. But so what? Maybe Rocco Lee, her new investment guru, was a smoker and wanted to cover up the stench. He was just trying to make a good impression.

"So, Miss Sheppard," Rocco Lee said as he accepted her check. "You will not be disappointed."

"I'm sure I won't," Ali said with a smile. "Tell me again exactly what I'm investing in."

She was no fool. She asked the tough questions. Ali even

□□□□□□□□□□□□□□□□□□□□□□□□□□□□□
11 Borrowed from Celeste.

pulled out a notebook and pen so she could write it down. Not responsible? Ha!

Rocco Lee folded his bizarrely hairy fingers on the metal desk in front of him and smiled a toothy grin. His curly salt-and-pepper hair was slicked back on the sides and a little bushy on top. It made Ali think of the *Laverne & Shirley* reruns her friend Wendy's mother used to watch on *Nick at Nite*. She wasn't sure why.

"Your much appreciated investment will be financing the capitalization of a new film company called Multiple Partners Pictures," Rocco explained, pushing up the sleeves of his somewhat shiny gray suit jacket. "You should quadruple your investment within two months."

Ali grinned. Quadruple. She loved that word. Quadruple. She hadn't had the guts to invest all of her father's money, so she'd just put in half—three thousand dollars. When it quadrupled she'd have twelve thousand. See, she was actually kind of good at math. Why couldn't they talk about investing dollars and cents in math class instead of useless *x*'s and *y*'s that didn't mean anything to anybody?

"Great! Well . . . I guess you'll contact me when the money starts rolling in, right?" Ali said, standing.

"Abso-freakin-lutely," Rocco said, pushing himself out of his chair. "It was nice to meet you, Alison Sheppard," he said as he offered his hand.

"You too, Rocco Lee," Ali returned, shaking with him. "Hey! Your name rhymes with broccoli."

"Yeah? Well, your name rhymes with . . . " He stopped,

unable to think of anything that rhymed with Allison Sheppard. "Ah, forget it," he said with a dismissive hand wave as he sat down again. "I'll be in touch."

Ali walked on air all the way back to campus. She was so happy she even decided to give the library another try. She was determined to get on track and start studying.

Ali breezed through the front door of Allween and slapped her ID card down on the security desk like an old pro. This was going to be no problem. If she could figure out how to sensibly invest her money, then she could figure out the Dewey decimal system.

But first things first. She had to score a table next to some cute guys. There was no reason why she couldn't do two things at once—study and earn some letters for the AHUL.

Ali roamed around for a while until she saw a guy she recognized from her French class. Perfect! She even had a built-in ice breaker. She went over to introduce herself.

"Hey! You're in my French class," she said.

"I know," he replied, beaming at her with eyes greener than any she'd ever seen. "You were awesome doing that translation and humiliating Schwartz like that."

"Hey, thanks, dude," Ali said, smiling. "I'm Ali Sheppard."

"I know that, too. I'm Liam Scott."

An *L*! Unbelievable. That was next on her list. This was turning into the most perfect day ever. This guy was adorable with a capital *L*. He was tall, with short curly red hair and pale freckles, and he looked like he did about a million sit-ups a day.

"Hey, you wouldn't be interested in possibly helping me with my French, would you?" she asked, lowering herself into the chair across from his. She really needed the help. It was probably her only hope of passing.

"Sure," he said, smiling at her. "Let's get some beginner books from the stacks and start with those."

"Uh, what are those?" she asked.

"Beginner books?" he asked, rising from the table.

"No, stacks."

"Oh boy," Liam said. "Well, they're rows and rows of dimly lit bookshelves where nobody ever goes."

"Oh, right. I've been there," she said as she followed him toward the elevators.

When they got to the French section, Liam pulled a book off the shelf like it was nothing. Like the Dewey decimal system was his native language.

"See, this one's perfect," Liam said. "It's a French kids' book called *Caroline et Bruno*. It has simple sentence structure, so it will be good to learn with."

"Great," Ali said, standing close to him and pretending to be totally interested. The picture showed a little French girl and a little French boy feeling very sleepy[12] and lying down. "Hey, I have a good idea. Why don't I be Caroline and you be Bruno?" Ali asked.

She lay down on the carpeting and grabbed his hand, pulling him down next to her. Then she took the book and

---

12 *Très fatigué.*

read aloud. *"Bonjour,* Bruno. *Je m'appelle* Caroline *et je suis très fatigué."*

"Uh, *bonjour,* Caroline. *Je m'appelle* Bruno *et je ne suis pas très fatigué,"* he said, smiling devilishly.

"What does that mean?" Ali asked.

"It means, Caroline . . . I mean, Ali, that I am *not* tired at all," Liam said.

The next thing she knew, he was kissing her. They were lying on their sides, on the floor, in the library, making out. He pulled her closer, and she could feel he had some major swelling going on in his jeans. She wondered how you said *that* in French.[13]

"I hope you know you're currently making out with a very wealthy dude," Ali whispered.

"Cool!" Liam said.

"Hey, how do you say dude in French?"

"I have no idea."

They started kissing again and he slipped his hand up her sweater and felt for her bra strap. "You know what else the stacks are called?" Liam asked.

"What?" Ali asked.

"Lovers' lanes."

And they were. A few feet away from them another guy and girl were seriously going at it, and in the next row, two girls were leaning against the stacks, making out like there was no tomorrow. Ali would have done this library thing a lot

13 *L'erection.*

sooner if she had known how much fun it was. It was like Amsterdam's Red Light District. In fact, they should have been in the Greek section instead of the French section, because even though they were French kissing, this was getting awfully close to being an orgy.

12

Two floors up, Jodi and Zack sat on piles of books and talked, like kids sitting on a haystack. They had been talking nonstop since their shift started two and a half hours ago. Only since it was the library, they had to whisper. And they had to sit pretty close to each other to do that.

"They're staring at us again," Jodi whispered.

"Who? The Russian Mafia?" Zack asked. They both looked down the row to see Serge and some guy named Vigo look away very quickly. "Just ignore them and they'll go away," Zack said.

"So wait, you actually had a sports-themed bar mitzvah?" Jodi said, returning to their conversation.

"Why is that so shocking?" Zack asked.

"You just don't seem like the sports type," Jodi replied with a shrug.

"Honestly, the only reason I had it was because my dad negged the astronomy theme I wanted," Zack whispered. "He was afraid I'd get my ass kicked behind the gym at school.

Science nerds were always getting their asses kicked back there."

Jodi giggled. The thought of Zack as a little brace-faced science nerd was just too cute.

"Why? What was your theme?" he asked, leaning back against the bookshelf behind him.

"It was a supermodel theme," Jodi admitted, flushing. Zack opened his mouth to mock her, but she slapped her hand over his lips before he could. "I've come a long way since then," she said.

He stuck out his tongue and licked her hand.

"Eeew!" she said, wiping her palm on her jeans. "Clearly *you* have not."

They both laughed, then fell into a comfortable silence. Jodi couldn't believe how easy it was to talk to Zack. They'd been sitting here for over an hour discussing everything from "garbage punch"[14] to sex, life, God, college, drugs, and what it meant to be a "modern Jew."

And she was getting paid to gab with this great guy! Although eventually, she figured, they would actually have to put some books on the shelves, because the Allween Library was starting to look like Filene's Basement after the last day of the annual sale.

Jodi looked down at her gold watch and frowned. "Hey, your shift was over like half an hour ago," she said.

"Yeah, well, I don't exactly feel like going home," Zack said, frowning.

□□□□□□□□□□□□□□□□□□□□□□□□□□□□

14 Take a big rubber garbage pail and fill it with any kind of juice and booze you can get your hands on until it's completely filled to the top.

"Why? Because sitting here with me is just that entertaining?" Jodi joked, hoping it actually *was* that entertaining for him.

"It beats dealing with the psycho roommate," Zack said, frowning.

It wasn't the most flattering answer, but it was an answer.

"Well, I'd better get some of these French books downstairs," Jodi said, her legs protesting as she rose. She'd definitely been sitting in the same position for a long time. "Got to earn that paycheck."

"Okay," Zack replied. "I'll see you around."

As Jodi made her way to the elevator, she felt really happy. She hadn't had that deep or interesting of a conversation with anyone, let alone a *guy*, in a good long time. Maybe ever. She was smiling as she hit the elevator button for the third floor.

When the doors slid open, she turned the corner and covered her mouth to keep from giggling. The only way she would be able to shelve the books would be to interrupt a couple of people who were lying on the floor making out. They were probably at that stage of dating where you really want to make out with the guy lying down, feeling the weight of his body on top of you, but you're not ready to have sex yet, so you don't want to go to his room or have him go to yours.

That was one of the most exciting stages of a relationship. Jodi suddenly felt incredibly sad, but she wasn't sure why. Because of Buster? Or maybe it was just the blatant reminder that she was critically behind in the AHUL. She was sure Ali was somewhere scoring letters as she stood there staring at a couple of strangers making out.

Jodi decided not to disturb the couple and shoved her books onto a random shelf. Then she turned and headed back to the fifth floor. *I'd better find my next letter soon*, she thought. *This is getting to be seriously depressing.*

13

"You're on *M*?!" Jodi exclaimed the next morning while she, Ali and Celeste were getting ready for class.

Ali shrugged as if it were no big deal, but she could tell from the disbelief in Jodi's voice and the fact that Celeste had gone pale that she was kicking ass at the Alphabetical Hookup List. She grinned as she pulled her black tank top on over her head. Winning the game, quadrupling her money, *and* up for class before 10 A.M. She was really getting a handle on things.

"Why? What letter are you on?" she asked.

Jodi swallowed, feeling like a reject. "I haven't even gotten my *E* yet."

Celeste perked up at this news. If Jodi had only gotten through *D* and she was going to get her *C* that afternoon, then she wasn't that far behind.

Suddenly there was a knock at the door. "UPS!"

"Oh God! What if it's Dirk?" Jodi said, shoving her arms into her cardigan.

"Maybe he won't remember you," Celeste said, hand on the doorknob. She knew this delivery was for her. Jib had promised her the pot would be here this morning.

"Right. Like any UPS dude would forget getting Frenched by a hot babe while making a drop-off," Ali said.

Jodi sat down at her desk with her back to the door, and Celeste signed for her package. It wasn't Dirk, but some scrawny guy with an actual eye patch.

"What's that?" Jodi asked when Celeste dropped the package on her bed without opening it.

"Oh, nothing," Celeste said, hoping her fibbing skills were improving. "Just a book I asked Jib to send me. I think it will help me with my music humanities class."

"Cool," Ali said, grabbing her bag. "Well, better get to class."

"Me too," Jodi added. "See you later, Celeste."

"Bye."

Celeste waited until their voices had faded down the stairwell at the end of the hall, then she ripped open the UPS box and pulled out a jumbo Ziploc bag of marijuana, two packs of E-Z Wider rolling papers, and a tin of butter cookies. Yum! Most college students would have been more psyched about the pot, but not Celeste. There was nothing better than Carla's butter cookies.

Celeste sat on her bed and piled all the paraphernalia in her lap, feeling more than a little nervous. Was this too much to take on at one time? Her first date with an older guy, her first smoke, *and* making sure she got a kiss for the AHUL?

What if she took one toke and threw up? What if Carter had no interest in kissing her whatsoever? What if he didn't even show? Celeste sighed and looked at the phone. Maybe she should at least confirm. . . .

Celeste moved her stuff aside and grabbed the phone before she could lose her nerve. She quickly dialed information.

"I'd like the number for Carter Mann," Celeste told the operator.

She was almost surprised when the operator gave it to her. It was almost like she had expected him not to exist—to just be a figment of her imagination.

Celeste held her breath and dialed the number. Her heart was racing by the third ring. Then a machine picked up.

"We're not in right now—please leave a message."

Celeste stood there in shock for a moment and then hung up. *We're. We. We're. We. We're not in right now.* Who was *we?* she wondered. A girlfriend? Was he married? Was she about to help this guy cheat on the woman in his life?

"Stop being so paranoid," Celeste told herself. "Maybe he just has a roommate or something."

She wasn't going to let her overactive imagination and even more hyperactive conscience get in the way of getting her *C.* One more after this and she could catch up to Jodi!

Celeste went to her closet and got dressed in the sexiest thing she had—a short black skirt, one-inch heeled sandals, and an almost tight, slim-strapped tank top. She had a contest to win, after all. Then she headed out to class.

14

By four o'clock Celeste was back in the triple, had made all three beds just in case Carter wanted to come upstairs, and was ready to shake apart from nerves. At exactly 4:01, she looked out the window, and there he was! Carter Mann was leaning against his car on the street below—a very sleek black Range Rover. Celeste smiled. In New York, guys didn't pick you up in their cars. They didn't even pick you up in cabs. They just sat in your lobby and waited for you to come downstairs and then made you walk about ten blocks to the subway. Or else you just sort of met somewhere.

Celeste grabbed her backpack. Pot—check. Rolling papers— check. Tears of a Clam matches—check. Butter cookies—check.

Carter grinned the moment he saw her emerge from Maize Hall, then he opened the passenger side door for her.

"Thanks," Celeste said as she melted into the lush leather seat. There really was something to this older guy thing. She might never date a guy her age again!

"Hey, I have a question," Celeste said as he started the car. "You don't have a girlfriend or a wife or anything, do you?" She kind of wanted to find out before she did yet another stupid thing with a guy.

"Nope. Just me and my dog, Sadie," Carter said, flipping down his visor to reveal a picture of an adorable black-and-white dog. "We live alone."

We. So that was what he meant on his machine when he'd said "we." He and his dog. Celeste didn't know if that was cute or lame.

"So did you bring the tape?" Carter asked as she pulled away from the curb.

"What tape?" Celeste asked. She'd been sure she managed to remember everything.

"The John Eltons," Carter said.

"Oh God, I forgot. I actually couldn't find the disc. I may have left it back home in New York, but I can probably have Jib send it to me." Damn, why did she have to mention her father? How immature.

"Who's Jib? Your boyfriend or something?" Carter asked.

He was asking her if she had a boyfriend. Was he trying to find out because he was hoping she didn't have a boyfriend, or because he was hoping she *did* have a boyfriend so this wouldn't be a date? Or was he just making polite small talk?

Maybe she'd just lead him on a little to find out.

"Oh, Jib? He's just a guy back in New York. I wouldn't exactly call him my boyfriend." There. She hadn't actually lied. Her father *was* a guy in New York and she *wouldn't* call him her boyfriend.

"I'm sure there are a lot of Jib-type guys waiting for you back in New York," Carter said, and gave her a sidelong look that she was pretty sure qualified as "smoldering."

"So where are we going, anyway?" she asked, feeling very pleased with the way things were going so far.

"A little peach orchard I know about," he said with a slow smile.

A peach orchard. That sounded so romantic. Celeste tried to keep herself from grinning like a schoolgirl for the rest of the ride, but she could barely help it. It was amazing how quickly she'd gone from Andy the Bloated and his sneezing and wheezing through *Gone With the Wind*, and a drunken night she couldn't even remember with Buster, to a romantic stroll with a hot older man. It was all she could do to keep from patting herself on the back.

Carter pulled the Range Rover into a dirt parking lot, and Celeste climbed down from the car. Her senses were immediately filled with the sweet scents of peaches and freshly cut grass from a nearby field where a few people were working. Carter walked toward a little shack with a painted sign that read *Fresh Peaches* and Celeste followed.

"Hey, Turk," Carter said to the wrinkled old man behind the window in the peach stand. "We're going to go for a little walk."

"Feel free," Turk said, pressing his lips together in a smile.

"Come here often?" Celeste asked as they stepped over the chain that separated the lush trees from the parking lot. Maybe he brought freshman girls here all the time. Turk seemed to know who he was.

"It's really peaceful," Carter said by way of an answer.

Celeste sighed serenely and looked around. She couldn't argue with that. There was nothing even approaching this place in New York. Plump fruit hung low from every branch, and the whole place was bathed in a sort of sweet golden glow from the sinking sun. Celeste reached out and touched one of the silky leaves as she and Carter walked. Could there possibly be a more romantic place?

"So did you bring it?" Carter asked.

"What?" Celeste asked, startled out of her thoughts.

"You and I had a date to smoke a spliff."

Celeste loved the word date. She took the huge bag of pot out of her backpack.

"Whoa," Carter said. "You have to handle these things a little bit more delicately." He grabbed her hand and pulled her behind a tree, then plucked a peach from a low branch and handed it to her. She ate the peach while he rolled a joint for them. It was the most delicious peach she had ever tasted.

Carter lit the joint and took a toke. "This stuff is amazing," he said.

"Told ya," Celeste said.

He took another and then handed the joint to Celeste. For a moment she simply held it at arm's length.

Am I really going to do this? she asked herself.

Yes.

It was time. *High* time, so to speak. After all, she'd been experiencing a lot of firsts lately.

Celeste took a hit and, thank God, she didn't cough. She handed the joint back to Carter.

"This is so great," he said. "With this stuff you could wake and bake all day."

"Yeah," she said, even though she had no idea what he was talking about. She took another hit off the joint. And then another. Then it started to hit her.

Celeste had known the pot would make her "high," but she had no idea what that would feel like. She figured she might get a little light-headed, but what she hadn't anticipated was that she would start giggling. And once she started, really be unable to stop.

As she giggled, she started to think of those two girls she had overheard talking to that guy about the fact that he didn't wear underwear. The more she thought about that guy not wearing underwear and the more she tried not to giggle, the more she actually giggled. She hadn't realized just how powerful Jib's pot was.

Finally she managed to stop thinking about the guy with no underwear long enough to realize that she and Carter had been together for well over an hour and he had made no attempt to kiss her. The only thing his lips looked like they wanted to touch was the end of that joint.

What if he'd only gone out with her for Jib's pot?

"Damn, this is the shit," Carter said, holding in his smoke and looking at the dwindling joint.

See! He really *had* only gone out with her for the pot!

"You know, you really remind me of this girl I dated back at school," Carter said, eyeing her.

Celeste smiled slowly. Okay, so maybe it *wasn't* just Jib's pot.

"God, that was ages ago," Carter said. "I really loved her."

Wait a second, what if he'd only gone out with her because she looked like this girl he'd loved? Maybe it wasn't her he wanted. Maybe he wanted to fuck some girl who looked like this ex of his and then dump her. Hold on. . . . Her mind was racing. What if—

But wait, had he said *ages* ago? How many ages? Maybe he'd only said it *seemed* like ages ago.

Everything was getting very confusing.

"You're so lucky, Celeste," Carter said. "You have all of that ahead of you."

"All of what?" Celeste said, managing to make one thought coherent.

"Well, actually, what they say is true."

"And what is that, President Carter?" Celeste asked, starting to giggle again.

"Life really does begin at thirty," Carter said.

Okay. Back up! Huh?

"How old *are* you?" Celeste asked. She reached out her hand and grasped his arm for balance. For the first time, she noticed that he had crumbs all over his shirt.

And why are you eating so many of Carla's butter cookies?

"I'm thirty-eight," Carter answered between mouthfuls. "But people always think I look a lot younger."

"WHAT!?" Celeste blurted.

He dropped the butter cookies to the ground and covered her mouth. "Shhh!" he said, his eyes huge and paranoid.

Celeste pulled away and buried her face in her hands. This guy was twenty years older than she was. He was old enough to be her dad. In fact, he was only a few years younger than Jib! This was so weird, maybe she would actually have to cross out his name on the list.

Of course even if she went through with it, he wouldn't be the oldest man in the AHUL. Ali had those three guys from the old age home on hers. But geez! Thirty-eight!

Suddenly this date wasn't sophisticated any more. It was all sort of, well . . . sleazy.

And Celeste was really pretty stoned.

"You don't look so good," Carter said.[15] "Maybe we should head back."

They didn't talk or giggle much on the ride home, just ate the cookies that hadn't fallen out of the tin when he'd dropped them.

When they pulled up in front of Maize, Carter asked if she would mind if he rolled one for the road.

Celeste just shrugged.

He rolled himself another fat joint, and then she grabbed

15 Last thing in the world you want to hear on a date.

what was left in the Ziploc bag, and the empty tin from the cookies. She wanted to send it back home so her mom could fill it up again and send it back to her now that Carter had basically eaten or ruined 90 percent of them.

"I had a really good time," Carter said.

"Yeah . . . bye," Celeste said. She wasn't even thinking about kissing him.

She got out of the SUV, stumbling a little as she did so. Had the Range Rover somehow grown a lot bigger since she got into it? It sure seemed like a long way down to solid earth.

Carter was old and frankly, a bit of a jerk. Celeste was high and frankly, a bit sick. But that wasn't the worst of it. When she got back to her room, she realized she had somehow left her backpack somewhere—probably under that tree in the peach orchard.

She knew there was a reason she'd never gotten high in high school.

15

The following morning, sitting in the back of her favorite class, Intro to Filmmaking, Jodi couldn't stop obsessing about the Alphabetical Hookup List. Or, more specifically, how well Ali was doing on the Alphabetical Hookup List. Jodi couldn't believe she was losing. When they had started the AHUL, she had thought she would be to *Z* and back three times over already by now. What the hell was taking her so long?

"Now, when you choose a project, you must choose a subject you truly care about," Professor Potter said, pacing back and forth at the front of the lecture hall.

Jodi sighed, tapping her pen against her blank notebook page. What she cared about was winning the Alphabetical Hookup List contest. And she *was* going to find a way.

At that moment she decided to give herself a goal of five. She would try to kiss five guys in alphabetical order in one day. *E, F, G, H,* and *I* would be hers by sundown. She couldn't very well just waste her life away in a library, talking about the burning grounds in India and how good the baklava tastes in Morocco. It was totally cool talking to Zack, but she had a contest to win.

There were plenty of kiss-worthy candidates right in this very room. The place was packed with aspiring Steven Spielbergs, Michael Bays, Ang Lees, and Spike Lees.[16] And a lot of them were hot. Maybe some were even wannabe-actors. Jodi would much rather kiss a pseudo-Heath Ledger than a young George Lucas.

Suddenly Jodi had a brilliant idea. It couldn't fail.

"Uh, can I make an announcement?" she asked Professor Potter, right before class was about to end.

"Sure," he said.

Jodi stood as every pair of eyes in the lecture hall turned to look up at her in the last row.

"I'm actually making a short film of my own—kind of a romance—and I need some, you know, actors to, you know, act in it. Just guys!" she said when she saw a couple of girls exchange looks of interest. "All the female roles are cast. Anyway, if anyone here is interested in auditioning, could you stay behind after class and we can set up an audition time? Oh, and I really only need your first names."

"Thank you, Miss Stein," Professor Potter said as Jodi sat down again. "It's nice to see a student take such initiative."

You better believe I'm taking initiative, Jodi thought. She

16 Two very different directors named Lee.

wrote "Auditions for *The Perfect Kiss*" across the top of her notebook and put it in front of her on the desk. The girls in the class started filing out the door, and she lost a few guys as well, but most of them stayed. One really weird-looking guy with a lot of piercings gave her a look of disdain as he passed by. Obviously not a fan of romantic films. Jodi wasn't sad to see him go.

The guys approached Jodi and started writing their names in her notebook. She smiled at each new prospect, quite proud of this little plan.

"Okay," she announced once everyone had signed in. She sounded extremely professional and official. "I don't have time to audition everyone today, so I'm going to call out five names. Would the five people I call please stay behind to audition now, and everyone else will be notified by phone about when the next auditions will take place." She took a deep breath and stared down at the list. "Elliot. Fela. Greg. Harrison. Izzy," she said.

"Cool," someone said.

"If your name wasn't called, please don't worry, I'll be calling you in the next few weeks," Jodi said. The rest of the guys filed out and Jodi looked at her five soon-to-be-kissed boys. Not a bad group.

"Okay, Elliot first," Jodi said.

"I don't want to go first," a shy blond boy said.

"I'm sorry, but you have to audition in the order in which your name was called," Jodi said. After all, the rule was that the kissing had to be done in alphabetical order.

Elliot reluctantly approached Jodi. "What do I have to do?" he asked, looking embarrassed.

"You just have to kiss me," she said.

The other four guys moronically high-fived each other.

"Huh?" Elliot asked, blanching.

"I'm playing the romantic lead, and if we don't have chemistry, it won't work," Jodi explained. "Kissing is the best way to find out."

"Uh, okay," Elliot said. "Standing or sitting?"

"How would you be more comfortable?" she asked.

"I don't know. Either way, I guess."

"Okay, standing, then," Jodi said. She marched over to him, tilted her head to the side, and kissed him. He did all kinds of things like dart his tongue in and out of her mouth really fast. A valiant effort, but *ick*.

"Okay, that was great," Jodi said, making Elliot blush. "Next is . . . ."

"I'm next," a gorgeous black guy said, looking extremely eager. He had dreds tied back with a bandanna, and luscious, kissable lips.

"You must be Fela," she said.

She walked over to him, and they kissed for twice as long as she had kissed the first guy. When it was over she was completely out of breath.

"Okay, then," Jodi said. "Maybe we'd better try that again. Fela, take two." She kissed him again and her knees almost went out from under her. "Okay, that was, um, outstanding," she managed to say when they parted. "Thank you."

Next came Greg and Harrison. Why hadn't she done something like this before? *Now* she was thinking. She wondered where Ali and Celeste would take her when she won the contest and got her prize—a great night out on the town in Atlanta!

Izzy was a little too aggressive for her taste. His kiss involved groping and was practically verging on date rape, or audition rape, or whatever, but he gave a convincing and compelling performance.

"Well, thanks for your time," Jodi said as she broke free from him. She smiled at the five guys. "I'll be in touch!"

The guys walked away and Jodi took out her Alphabetical Hookup score sheet. She proudly wrote down the five names, bringing her all the way to *J*.

"Do you have time for one more?" someone asked from behind her.

Jodi whirled around, startled, to find a very Buster-like guy standing at the other end of her row of seats. He had a broad chest, sandy brown hair, hazel eyes, and slanting eyebrows, kind of like Christian Slater. He even had a cast on his left arm[17] and was wearing a T-shirt that read *Body by Nautilus, Brains by Mattel.*

"Well, uh . . ."

"My name's Jared, and I'm really interested in auditioning," he said.

□□□□□□□□□□□□□□□□□□□□□□□□□□□□□
17 Buster had broken his leg.

Jared? Perfect! "Sure," Jodi said. She took the cap back off her pen and added Jared to the list.

"How did you break your arm?" she asked.

"Skateboarding," he said.

"I like your eyebrows," she told him.

"Oh—it's kind of an embarrassing story," Jared said, looking at the floor.

"What is?" Jodi asked.

"Well, my ex-girlfriend waxed them," he explained. "I think they look weird."

"I think they're nice," she said.

Now *this* was a guy she really could fall in love with. *Should* fall in love with. He was a normal guy—sweet and normal.

Jared leaned down and kissed her, and she rested her hand on his cast and kissed him back. He was a really good kisser. Not too eager. Not too shy. Just the right amount of tongue. And he had the softest lips. Unlike Zack.

Zack? I refuse to think of Zack, Jodi told herself. She pressed her body closer to Jared's, and he wrapped his good arm around her. *It doesn't matter that he didn't kiss me back.* This *guy is definitely into kissing me.*

Suddenly a mental image of Zack in the library, licking her hand, flitted into her mind. And before she knew it, he was licking a lot more than her hand. She deepened the kiss with Jared, and he moaned and leaned back against the seat behind him.

Jared. I'm kissing Jared, Jared, Jared.

And then, in her mind, Zack was pulling off her shirt and she couldn't take it anymore. She broke away from Jared so suddenly, he almost fell backward over the lecture hall seat. She grabbed his shoulders just in time.

"Sorry," Jodi said, her lips stinging.

"Don't apologize," Jared said. His eyes were glassy. Clearly she'd had an effect.

"So, I'll call you about the film," Jodi said, quickly gathering her stuff.

She turned and fled the building, gulping in some fresh air. What was happening to her? How could she be making out with a totally hot guy—and thinking about Zack? Could she actually be falling in love with him?

Please, no, Jodi thought, heading across the quad. She could not fall in love with a guy who only wanted to be her friend. Not only would it turn her whole life upside down, but it would seriously screw up her AHUL goal.

Z was a long way away.

16

Ali stood on a crowded street corner and considered the task at hand. This had to be one of the most moronic things she had ever had to do, but she was really trying to stop screwing up, and social psych was one of her worst classes.

She was supposed to be performing an experiment: Drop some quarters on the ground, first in a crowded area and then in a secluded area, and see if people were less likely to pick up money where there was an audience.

She really needed her quarters for laundry, so she tried it with a Canadian penny. No one stooped to pick it up. There was even this homeless dude wandering around who didn't bother to stop—which proved pretty much nada, except that no one stops for pennies, Canadian or otherwise.

Ali sighed. She was going to have to come up with *something* to give her social psych lab or they were going to kill her. She hadn't really pulled her weight at all yet.

She took out her yellow Paul Frank monkey wallet and grabbed a five-dollar bill. What the hell? She'd be rich soon, and her father would be proud that she'd spent his money on a school project.

She dropped the five near the bus stop and hung back by the window of a nearby deli to watch. About three seconds later a skinny guy wearing a denim vest over his bare chest picked up the five, put it in his pocket, and kept walking. He didn't look especially guilty or anything, just happy that he had found a five-dollar bill. Maybe he was going to use it to buy a cheap T-shirt.

This really was bullshit. This was what all that tuition money was paying for—standing on the street and waiting for people to pick up money?

Resisting the urge to go back to Maize Hall and do something more interesting like tweeze her brows, Ali walked for a while and found a secluded spot. It was a small patch of grass with a couple of trees and three benches set up in a triangle. This time Ali decided to invest only one dollar. She put it on the ground near the benches, and then walked away and leaned against the farthest tree.

She waited, hoping someone would come along. As homework went, it wasn't exactly strenuous. Ali kind of felt like a spy. Maybe she would get a job as a PI one day.

It really could have been a lot worse. The people in the other lab had to pretend to faint in the middle of crowded areas to see who was more likely to help—men or women. Actually, Ali thought, that would have been better for the AHUL. She could just lie there and hope a man with the right first name would show up and give her mouth to mouth. Mouth to mouth would definitely count.

Finally a big fat dude came loping along. He was eating a Subway hero, but it definitely wasn't the kind with less than six grams of fat in it. He didn't exactly look like he was going to be the new poster boy for the Subway Diet.[18]

Fatman saw the dollar and stopped. He stood there, staring at it. Then he looked around to see if anyone was nearby. Finally he picked it up. He started walking in the direction of Ali's tree. He was wearing a big, baby-blue bowling shirt with the name *Mooner* embroidered over the pocket.

When he saw her he said, "Hey, did you lose a dollar?"

The dude was totally fucking with her hypothesis.

On the other hand, his name began with *M*, and Ali was up to *M*. . . .

"Uh, maybe," she said.

"You want it back?"

"I guess so," Ali said.

Here was the real experiment: Are you more likely to kiss guys you are totally unattracted to in a secluded environment or a crowded one in order to win the AHUL? Hypothesis: The threat of embarrassment will be overcome by the desire to win.

"Is your name really Mooner?" Ali asked.

"Yeah!" Mooner said, grinning. "Well, it's actually a nickname, but that's what everyone calls me. Because I love to moon people."

"Oh, that's great," Ali said.

"Really?" Mooner said.

□□□□□□□□□□□□□□□□□□□□□□□□□□□□

18 Referring to a man who admitted to losing more than a hundred pounds by eating Subway's veggie and turkey heroes. He did a national ad campaign.

Yeah, Ali thought. Nicknames counted if they were official and the person was commonly known by that nickname. This guy's was official enough to be stitched on his shirt.

"I think I did lose that dollar," Ali said.

"Here," he said, handing it to her.

"Hey, dude, how can I thank you?" Ali asked.

"Oh you don't have to thank me," Mooner said. He had a piece of shredded lettuce hanging out of the corner of his mouth. Why was it that some people couldn't *feel* when they had food on their face?

"Well, at least let me give you a thank-you kiss."

Mooner looked at her wide eyed, like a cartoon dog.

"Uh . . . "

She stood on her tiptoes and gave him a long, soft kiss, after removing the lettuce strand.

"Thanks," she said.

"No, thank *you.*" He leaned in to kiss her again, but she ducked down and managed to escape his embrace.

"Whoa, dude, it was only a buck," she said. "See ya."

She started to walk away, but she heard him call out, "Hey!" and she turned around.

All she saw was his enormous white ass. He was bent over, pulling his cheeks apart with his hands. He had one red zit right smack in the middle of his left cheek.

Now *that* was what she should write her final paper on for social psych. Mooning. Obviously it was a very interesting social phenomenon that really needed to be explored.

17

"My life sucks," Celeste said to the empty dorm room. She lay back on her bed.

She'd woken up that morning with a monster headache and immediately recalled the ridiculous so-called date with Carter the day before. Once she thought of him, she couldn't help but think of her ridiculous so-called date with Andy the Bloated and her night of unremembered passion with Buster. What the hell was the Alphabetical Hookup List doing to her?

"It's turning you into a raving lunatic *and* the campus slut," Celeste muttered, resting her hand on her still-throbbing forehead. It had also gotten her backpack lost for her. That was the last straw. It had to stop. Right now. She had to stop trying to accomplish this hideous goal.

It wasn't like she was getting anywhere on the list, anyway.

Suddenly the phone rang, and Celeste sat up way too fast, sending a dart of pain through her temple. Grimacing, she checked the caller ID. *Private number.* At least it wasn't Andy or Carter. Or worse—Buster. Celeste picked up the phone.

"Celeste Alexander?" a thick voice asked.

"Yes?"

"This is campus security. We have your backpack. You'd better come down and—"

Celeste didn't even wait to hear the end of his sentence. She was out the door and running across campus before the security guy realized there was no one on the other end of the line.

"You're a very lucky lady," the security guard said when Celeste arrived and explained who she was.

"Thanks," Celeste said, relieved to see her bag as he pulled it off a shelf behind him. She was very lucky that there was no pot left in there, that was for sure.

"I hope you'll be just a little more careful next time, young lady," the security guy said with an all-knowing smirk.

"Young lady?" Celeste repeated. The security guy barely looked any older than she was—not that she was the best judge of age these days. His badge said *Junior Security Officer Craig Brown.* She hated when people said you were lucky. And she hated patronizing twerps. But at the same time Celeste couldn't help noticing that Craig began with a *C.*

"Yes, sirree, if I were you, I'd thank my lucky stars that some good citizen found this and turned it in." He was still holding her backpack. "What were you doing in a peach orchard, anyway, if you don't mind my asking?"

Celeste grabbed her bag. "You really want to know what I was doing in that peach orchard, Junior Security Officer Craig Brown?" she asked. "I was smoking pot and making love!"

She took his head in her hands and kissed him really fast, and then ran like crazy to get the hell out of there.

When she had run as far as she could without collapsing, she fell back on a bench and tried to get over the shock of what she had just done. She felt more like a combination of Ali and Jodi than herself. Her resolution to give up the AHUL sure hadn't lasted long. Old habits died hard, she supposed. But that was it, she promised herself. Her list was ending on *C*, and that was final.

Feeling strangely proud, she opened her bag to make sure everything was still there, and it was—even the money in her wallet and her emergency credit card. Relieved, Celeste opened her Filofax to add Security Junior Officer Craig Brown and cross out Pot-head Pervert Carter Mann from her hookup list. Her pen was poised over the page when she noticed it was crinkled. In fact, a couple of the pages in her planner were crinkled. Huh. Had Junior Security Officer Craig Brown gone through her planner? Ugh. Suddenly she felt slimy. Wasn't that an invasion of privacy or something?

Celeste flipped the Filofax closed, but as she did, she suddenly realized that she'd written her name, campus address and phone number on the first page, in case the planner was lost. Of course! They had probably looked through it for her info. It was easier than looking her up in the massive campus directory.

Shaking her head at her paranoia, Celeste headed back to the dorm. Maybe there was still a little bit of that pot left in her system.

18

"Ms. Sheppard?" the pinch-faced student receptionist said from behind her massive desk. "The dean will see you now."

Ali yanked down on the front of her mesh sweater and wiped her palms on her skirt. She still had no idea why Dean Redding wanted to see her. She had been obsessing about it since the moment she'd found a notice in her mailbox earlier that day "inviting" her to a "mandatory meeting." She knew she was doing poorly in her classes, but they hadn't even gotten grades yet. Dean Redding couldn't be planning to boot her out, could she?

Ali stepped into an overly air-conditioned office decorated with gleaming birch-wood furniture and floral patterns. A middle-aged woman in a blue suit stood up from behind an impeccably clean desk.

"Alison Sheppard?" the dean said with a kind smile. "Have a seat." She gestured at one of the two huge leather chairs across the desk.

Ali smiled back. Maybe this wasn't going to be bad news.

Nobody was ever that serene and happy before delivering bad news.

Suddenly a little beeper went off somewhere in the room.

"Excuse me," the dean said. She turned and opened a cabinet with about five prescription bottles inside and popped a tiny pill. Then she turned back again, smiling a serene and happy smile.

"Ms. Sheppard," the dean said, folding her hands on her desk. "I'm sorry to have to tell you that you are being placed on academic probation."

All said with a nice wide grin.

"What?" Ali said, horrified. "How?"

"We ask all the professors to make us aware of any students who seem to be on the wrong track early in the semester," the dean said, her eyes dancing. "This way we can meet with those students and evaluate whether or not Pollard is really the place for them."

Whether or not Pollard was the place for her? Holy shit. They *were* booting her.

"I know I haven't been . . . living up to my potential," Ali said, hoping her professorial language made her sound thoughtful and mature.

Redding pulled a slim manila folder across the desk and opened it. "Apparently you're not meeting that potential in French . . . social psychology . . . Introduction to Feminist Thought. It says here that Professor Hickerson isn't even sure she's ever set eyes on you." The dean's eyes flicked over Ali's outfit, then settled on her nose ring. "And I think she'd have a hard time forgetting."

Ali flushed. "So, what do I have to do?" she asked, gripping her armrests.

"I suggest you get to work and bring up some of these grades," the dean said placidly, closing the folder again. "At the end of the semester we'll talk again and decide on your future here at Pollard."

Or nonfuture, Ali thought, reading between the lines. She could barely lift herself out of the chair. What the hell was wrong with her? How had she let it get so bad?

She walked out of the dean's office in a fog, barely noticing which direction she was heading. When she finally looked up, she was walking past International House. Posters of famous international landmarks plastered the big, plate-glass front windows: the Eiffel Tower, the Colosseum, the Buddhist temple at Angkor Wat, the Forbidden City.

Ali stopped and stared at the posters. At that moment, even a Buddhist temple sounded like a better place to be than Pollard University. *Maybe I should just use the rest of my tuition money to buy a plane ticket,* she thought. *I could go somewhere and never come back.*

But then she'd have to say good-bye Jodi and Celeste. That would be sad.

Sighing, Ali started walking again.

What was she going to do?

19

Celeste was sitting in the Maize Hall lounge, reading *The Beauty Myth* for Intro to Feminist Thought, when suddenly someone covered her eyes from behind.

"Guess who, dude?" a voice asked.

"Ali?"

Sure enough, Ali climbed over the back of the battered couch and flopped down next to Celeste.

"Hey, dude," Ali said with a sigh.

"Hey, dude," Celeste said back. She had never thought she would get used to Ali's dude thing, but she was.

Ali was usually bursting with energy, but now she was slumped so far down in the couch, she was becoming one with the cushions. "What's wrong?" Celeste asked, putting her book down between them.

"I just met with Dean Redding," Ali said.

"Why?" Celeste asked.

"I guess I've sort of . . . fallen behind in a few classes," Ali said, flicking her eyes toward Celeste, then looking down again. "She gave me a talking-to, if you know what I mean."

"That's terrible," Celeste said. "But it doesn't sound too bad, right? They probably just wanted to see if everything was okay. They're touchy-feely like that around here."

"Actually, she said that if I don't get my act together soon, I'll be taking it on the road," Ali said, picking at her fingernails.

"You mean leave PU?" Celeste asked, her heart dropping. It had never occurred to her that one of them would leave.

"Sucks, huh?" Ali said with a wry smile. "And I was doing so well with the AHUL."

"Fuck the AHUL," Celeste said.

This time Ali smiled for real. "Did Celeste Alexander just say the word *fuck*?"

"You bet your ass I did," Celeste said, sitting up straight. Ali laughed and sat up herself. "I am not going to let you flunk out of school," Celeste added firmly.

"Oh, really?" Ali asked, raising her eyebrows.

"Yes, *really*," Celeste told her. "I'll help you."

"What do you want to help a fuckup like me for?" Ali asked.

"You're not a fuckup. You just fucked up," Celeste said. She kind of liked this *f*-word thing. She should use it more often. "Now, what's your worst class?"

"Intro to Feminist Thought," Ali said. "I don't even have the books."

"I didn't know you were taking that. So am I. Well, that makes it easy. Here," Celeste said, picking up *The Beauty*

Myth and handing it to Ali. "I'm ahead in the reading. Just borrow my books."

"Seriously?" Ali asked.

"Of course!" Celeste said. "And trust me, once you start reading that, you will not be able to put it down. That book is some seriously messed-up shit."

Ali laughed again. "You're starting to talk like me."

"And you're going to start studying like me," Celeste said.

Ali flipped through the first few pages of the book and looked up at Celeste, her eyes bright with gratitude.

"Thanks, C.," she said. She reached over and threw her arms around Celeste's neck. Celeste hugged her back.

"No problem," she said. "Don't worry. You're not going anywhere."

"I hope not," Ali said. But she didn't sound convinced.

20

Jodi, Celeste, and Ali were all feeling seriously depressed. Even though Celeste had offered to help Ali with her work, Ali wasn't able to erase the fear of failing and getting kicked out. And even though Celeste had gotten her bag back, she couldn't stop thinking about Carter and cringing. Jodi . . . well, Jodi was just thinking about Zack. They all lay on their beds in their triple, staring at the peeling paint on the ceiling and listening to a bad country station on the radio.[19]

"I think I kind of like country music," Jodi announced.

"Oh God! What the hell are you thinking?" Ali said.

"What? It's not all bad," Jodi said.

"It's pain," Celeste said seriously. "The music of pain."

Ali looked at Jodi, then at Celeste, and before they knew it, they had all cracked up.

Jodi sighed and picked up her *Cosmo*, and Celeste propped herself up on her elbow. She narrowed her eyes at

19 The only station they could get in the triple.

Jodi. It looked like there was some other magazine inside the *Cosmo*. Like Jodi was hiding something.

"What are you reading?" Celeste asked.

"Magazine," Jodi mumbled, and turned the page.

Celeste caught a glimpse of a wedding gown on the page as it was being turned. "What *is* that?" she squealed. She jumped up and grabbed the secret magazine. Her jaw dropped. *Modern Bride.*

Celeste read the whole cover out loud: "'It's Your Day—So Keep It That Way.' 'Dresses That Dazzle.' 'Our Favorite Favors—Life Beyond Jordan Almonds.'"

"It's not that big a deal," Jodi said, although she was totally mortified. Especially since she'd been secretly thinking about Zack while reading an article called "Ten Best Proposals Ever."

It would happen in the library. He would hand her a book. *What's this?* she would say. *It's the first book we shelved together,* he would say. She would open it, and there would be an overdue slip with the words, *Will you marry me?* written on it. The pouch that held the card with the date stamped on it would be bulging. (Okay, so there were no pouches or date cards in library books anymore, but a girl could dream.) In it would be a beautiful antique three-carat diamond ring.

"Dude, why are you reading a wedding magazine?" Ali asked. As much as she loved Jodi, sometimes her initial impression of Jodi as a total JAP was definitely validated.

"Well, Buster and I talked a lot about getting

married," Jodi said. "And one day I bought one of these stupid bridal magazines, you know, just to goof on it, and I sort of got hooked on them. It's kind of a secret obsession of mine."

"That's really weird," Ali said.

"You both have your secret obsessions," Jodi said.

"I do not," Ali said.

"Then *duuuude*, why are you here every single day no matter what watching *General Hospital*?"

"Touché," Celeste said, laughing.

"I wouldn't laugh if I were you," Jodi said, smiling. "I'm not the one with the *Kama Sutra* hidden under a *Saint Lucia* book jacket."

"And *The Happy Hooker* pretending to be *The Life of Saint Joan*," Ali added.

"All right, all right," Celeste said, blushing.

Celeste and Ali went back to studying, and Jodi went back to *Modern Bride*. She was kind of relieved her secret was out. Now she could just enjoy her magazines in the open.

"I got my *M*," Ali said, glancing at her friends for a reaction.

"I actually got six guys in one day," Jodi said nonchalantly. She didn't actually care, of course. She just wanted to be done with it so she could get to *Z*.

"What!?" Celeste said. "Six guys! How did you do that?" To Celeste that was like saying, "I just flew to the moon and back in one day."

"I don't know if I should tell the competition all my secrets," Jodi said with a smirk.

"So Jodi, what letter are you up to?" Ali asked.

"*K* is next," Jodi said. "Gotta find a *K*."

Celeste was really feeling miserable now. She was a complete and total failure at this. A fuckup, as Ali would say. This whole thing was getting her way too down, and she was tired of it.

Why don't I just lie? she thought suddenly. *Why am I even taking this so seriously?* For all she knew, *they* were lying. How could anybody get six guys in one day? It was impossible.

That was it. She was going to lie. It wasn't nice to lie to her friends, but she had to for her own self-esteem.

"All right, let's get out our lists," Ali said, like, *Let's get our guns,* or *Let's get our swords.* In other words, let the games begin!

"I'll get the drinks," Jodi said, leaving the room with her wallet.

"I'll get Buddha," Celeste said.

Buddha was the bronze statue of a jolly, fat-bellied Buddha that Jib had given Celeste on move-to-college-day. He was also a safety deposit box, and if you rubbed his stomach three times to the right, it opened and you could hide stuff in it. During the Great Jodi Bed Fire, Buddha had taken quite a licking, but he had survived from the neck down. Only his head had melted. Buddha had sort of become a symbol of the AHUL—a mascot, so to speak— because they hid the piece of loose-leaf paper that contained the "AHUL Amendments" inside him. They kept him in the closet but always brought him out when they had AHUL meetings.

"I'll be right back, Ali," Celeste said, depositing Buddha on the floor and grabbing her bag. "Nature calls."

Celeste scurried to the bathroom and pulled out the Filofax and her list. She quickly added six boys' names to it, bringing herself up to *J*. Feeling incredibly guilty, she looked at her reflection in the mirror and steeled her gaze. She had to do this. It was the only way to save face.

Back at the triple, Celeste, Ali, and Jodi sat in a circle with the melted-headed Buddha between them and six cans of Coke, Diet Coke, and Sprite at their sides. Jodi held up a bottle of rum. "Courtesy of lazy-eyed, narcoleptic K.J. Martin," she explained. "She still feels guilty about burning my bed."

"Excellent. Okay, Jodi, you first," Ali said. "Produce your list."

Jodi got her list and passed it to Ali and Celeste. It was filled with a lot of cross outs for the guys who had been deemed unacceptable and replaced with other names that were highlighted in yellow.

ALPHABETICAL HOOKUP LIST

A: *Zit-faced Alex*

B: *Buster*

C: *Charlie*

D: ~~*Druggie Steve + David Hasselhoff (I swear)*~~ *UPS Dirk*

E: ~~*Eric*~~ *Elliot*

F & G: ~~*Gross Fredo*~~ *Fela & Greg*

H: ~~*Jorge (pronounced Whore-hey) & Hotdog Truck Steve*~~ *Harrison*

I: ~~*Ian*~~ *Izzy*

J: ~~John (and Jorge)~~ *Jared*

K:

"Come on, how'd you get six guys in one day?" Ali asked. "It sounds like a story that we will one day tell our grandchildren. The day Jodi Stein made AHUL history."

"All right, I'll tell you if I have to," Jodi said. "It actually took less than half an hour."

Way to make me feel worse, Celeste thought.

Jodi took a deep breath. "I made an announcement in my film class that I was making a romantic film and I needed actors for it. Everyone wrote their names down, and then I auditioned six of them in alphabetical order—the next six letters I needed. I kissed each and every one of them."

"So you tricked them into thinking they were going to be in a movie?" Celeste asked. "That's so mean!"

"It's genius," Ali proclaimed, feeling jealous, but genuinely proud of her friend. "Here's my list," she said, pulling it out of her desk drawer, where it was folded into quarters.

Jodi poured herself a decent shot of rum in a glass and added some Diet Coke. Then she unfolded Ali's list and looked through it.

THE ALPHABETICAL THINGY GAME

~~A: Amelia~~	A: *Antonio*
~~B: Barbara~~	B: *Brian*
~~C: Chris~~	C: *Captain Morgan*
~~D: Diane~~	D: *Don the drummer from the Athens Greeks*

E: ~~Eve~~   E: *Nice Ed*

F: ~~Frieda~~   F: *Frank from retirement home*

G: ~~Guinevere~~   G: *George from retirement home*

H: ~~Hallie Tosis~~   H: *Harry from retirement home*

I: ~~Ian~~   I: *Ian Haas (had sex with)*

J: ~~Jennifer~~   J: *Cute Jason*

K: *Karl the mail-room guy*

L: *Liam*

M: *Mooner (fat guy who gave me dollar)*

"Well, that certainly is impressive," Celeste said, looking at Ali's list and feeling a little sick. These girls were willing to do anything to win. Hold fake movie auditions? Kiss a fat guy who gave you a dollar? These were just not things that Celeste would ever bring herself to do. Carter had been old, but at least he hadn't been in a retirement home. Celeste didn't want to seem immature, but . . . *eeew.*

"So far I'm winning," Ali said. "Despite my setback with the Lesbian Alliance. Okay, Celeste, let's see yours. Oh, and by the way rum and Sprite sucks." She tossed off the last of her drink and made a face.

Celeste took out her Filofax (Jodi had copied the idea of keeping it in a Filofax from her) and produced the list.

THE COLLEGE MEN OF CELESTE ALEXANDER
(IN ALPHABETICAL ORDER)

A—Andy the Bloated

B—Buster (worst mistake of my life)

C—Junior Security Officer Craig Brown
D—Dante
E—Elmo
F—Fuzzy
G—George
H—Hyronimous
I—Ivan

Jodi and Ali looked down at the list in disbelief.

"Who are these people?" Jodi asked. "Who has names like Hyronimous and Dante?"

"Celeste, did you kiss Elmo from *Sesame Street*? Did he close his big googly eyes?" Ali asked. "Did you run your fingers through his red fur?"

"And can we discuss for a moment kissing a man named *Fuzzy?*" Jodi asked.

"Fuzzy's great," Celeste said, lamely.

"Who is Ivan?" Jodi asked, earnestly.

"Just a guy," she said. She was sort of panicking because she hadn't really expected to receive the third degree.

"What's his last name?" Ali asked.

"McKean," Celeste said, spewing the first last name that came into her head.

"Ivan McKean!" Jodi shrieked. "*Professor* Ivan McKean? Your Music Humanities teacher? Whoa, Celeste."

Celeste's heart froze midthump. She couldn't believe she'd just said that! How could she have just said that?

"Dude!" Ali said, jumping up from her cross-legged position

on the floor in one motion like some kind of super-Yogi. "Way to come out of your shell."

Celeste sat frozen on the floor, racking her brain for a way to get out of this. Unfortunately, she came up blank. Hand shaking, she poured herself a glass of rum to stall for time.

Jodi put her arm around Celeste. "Ali," she said, pretending to be teary eyed. "I think our little baby's growing up."

"Yeah," Ali said, "she's a regular Lolita."

"Sooooo?" Jodi said.

"So what?" Celeste asked, sipping her drink.

"So, tell us everything. What was it like to kiss Professor McKean? How did it happen? What did you say? Did you come on to him or did he come on to you? We have to know the whole story. Because *this* really *is* AHUL history."

Despite her completely panicked state, before she knew it, Celeste had made up an entire story. Professor McKean had asked a really hard question, and she had answered it correctly. *Ivan*, as Celeste was now calling him, was so impressed, he asked her to stay after class so he could congratulate her. Then one thing had led to another, and that was that.

"Whoa," Jodi said. "What do you mean, one thing led to another, and that was that? Details, please."

"I don't know," Celeste said. "There's not that much to tell. Ivan and I just had a really nice conversation, and he sort of complimented me a lot and said I was one of the best students he had ever had, and then I told him what a good teacher he was and, well, we just had really good chemistry together."

Ali and Jodi's eyes were so wide, they were starting to

resemble Elmo's. This was a whole new Celeste. "So how did the kiss actually happen?" Jodi asked. "It *was* just a kiss, wasn't it?"

"Oh yeah, definitely," Celeste said quickly.

"How did it happen?" Ali prodded.

"Well, I had to go to my next class and he thanked me for staying late and then, um, he kissed me." For a moment she had been tempted to add a part where Professor McKean told her how beautiful and sexy and hot she was, but she just couldn't bring herself to do it.

"Oh my God," Jodi said, downing the rest of her rum cocktail.

"Oh, my dudey dudey dude," Ali said.

"Yeah," Celeste said. "Just don't tell anyone, okay?"

Celeste, Jodi, and Ali looked at each other, realizing the immense secrecy that had to be maintained for their little game. And now that they were advancing in letters, the pressure was really starting to build.

"So, this is one close competition," Ali said, leaning back against the side of her bed. She had thought she was home free, but Jodi and Celeste weren't that far behind. "We are racking up the guys."

"Yeah. Pollard University had no idea what they were getting when they accepted us," Jodi said.

"A bunch of sluts," Celeste said under her breath.

They all exchanged a glance and then dissolved into laughter all over again.

21

Later that evening Jodi arrived for a shift at the library to find Zack already hard at work. The Russian Mafia, thank God, had cleared out. They were alone, and the library was about to close for the night. She and Zack were working past closing to shelve the huge numbers of books the Russian Mafia had left lying on the carts.

"What's that on your face?" Zack asked, taking a moment to look up from what he was doing.

"What?" Jodi asked, alarmed. What the hell was on her face?

"I like when your face is its own normal, natural color. I mean, if God had intended lips to be purple he would have made them that way," Zack said.

Oh, so he meant her makeup. Great. Zack hated makeup. "Well, I don't care. I love wearing makeup," Jodi said. "And it's my God-given right as a woman."

"All right, be that way," Zack said with a shrug. "I can see you're in a difficult womanly mood."

Jodi sort of liked the idea of being in a difficult womanly mood. It sounded sort of mature and romantic in a Bob Dylanish, "Just Like a Woman" kind of way.

"I'm not in a difficult mood. I'm just a little tipsy," Jodi said.

"Oh, really?" Zack asked, grinning at her. "And what has my Jodi been imbibing today?"

My Jodi!

"Rum," Jodi said, smiling.

"Well then, I see I'll have to pull most of the weight."

He picked up a book, *The Complete Works of Oscar Wilde,* and pretended to be one of the Russians.

"Please to tell me, Joe-dee, where to go this?" he asked, a bemused expression on his face.

Jodi cracked up, loving the fact that he could make her laugh so easily.

"Try *W,*" she said, playing along.

"Double You?" Zack said in his phony Russian accent. He raised his eyebrows and fake-leered at her. "I would like to double *you.* Two Joe-dees better than one."

He walked by her with the book and pinched her side. Jodi yelped and then slapped her hand over her mouth, remembering where she was.

As Zack disappeared down one of the rows of books, Jodi tried to wipe the grin off her face but failed. This was one massive crush. God, she wished she could tell Ali and Celeste how she was feeling. She longed for hours of girl talk where she told them over and over again about everything that he had said to her. What they would think? Was there any chance that he liked her? What were the signs? Had the Ecstasy incident really done as much damage as she thought it had, or was it really behind them? These were questions only her friends could answer, and Ali and Celeste had become her best friends.

Unfortunately, they had sworn off relationships and dedicated themselves to the Alphabetical Hookup List. She couldn't back out on that now.

Jodi got so emotional thinking about how much she loved her friends that her eyes got teary. Man, she really shouldn't have had so much rum before coming to work.

"Hey, what's wrong?" Zack said, returning from the stacks. He looked at her, his brow creased with concern. "Jodi, are you crying?"

She wished she could just lay it on the line and tell Zack how she felt. Maybe she should. Even if he rejected her and didn't share her feelings at all, maybe it would be better just to know so she could try to think about something other than him.

"No," Jodi said. "I'm not crying. I think I just drank a little too much and I had sort of a weird day. I have a lot on my mind."

"Like what?" Zack asked.

"Oh, it's nothing. Just deep dark secrets of the soul."

"Tell me the deepest darkest one," Zack said with a small smile.

"I'm addicted to bridal magazines," Jodi said with a nod. "I secretly buy and read them every single month."

"Which is your favorite?" Zack asked, sounding completely unfazed.

"*Martha Stewart Weddings,*" Jodi said. "But it only comes out four times a year."

"That one's my favorite, too," Zack said with a sigh, putting his hands on his hips and shaking his head. "It's just such torture waiting for the next one to come out!"

"I know what you mean," Jodi played along with a little sniffle.

"Come here," Zack said, holding out his arms. "It'll be okay. There *will* be another issue."

Jodi laughed and stepped into his embrace. She loved the feeling of his arms around her, even if they were just joking around. Her mouth was close to his ear, and his hair smelled freshly shampooed.

"You use Herbal Essences," Jodi said, smiling.

"Yeah," Zack replied. "I like the name. Herbal Essences. You know, herbs make me think of really good weed. I just switched from Pantene. I like that name, too, because it sounds like panties."

Jodi giggled. Zack pulled away slightly.

"Don't hate me because I'm beautiful," he said.

Jodi laughed, and Zack let her go. Blushing, she turned and picked up the top book from one of the many piles around them. Even if she couldn't tell Zack how much she liked him, at least now she knew for sure how *she* felt. She definitely liked him. In fact, she probably loved him.

Zack dropped to the floor and started to sort the books, so

Jodi followed suit. They made piles of books to bring to different sections of the library, getting organized so that they wouldn't be there all night. Jodi enjoyed the quiet coziness between them as they worked.

"It's too quiet in here," Zack said suddenly.

"I kind of like it," Jodi replied.

"Want to play a game?" Zack asked.

Jodi placed a thick biochemistry book on the science pile and turned her attention to Zack. This was an intriguing suggestion. "Like what?"

"Like . . . we ask each other trivia questions and if you get one wrong, you have to kiss one part of my body—whichever I tell you to—and vice versa," Zack said as if it were the most normal suggestion in the world.

Jodi's cheeks reddened. "Wait a minute. I thought you just wanted to be friends," she said.

"I do. I'm just bored," Zack said.

Jodi stared hard at him. Did he really mean that? He couldn't possibly—could he? No. He wanted more, he just wasn't ready to admit it yet. Kind of like Jodi herself.

Right?

"Okay, I'm in," Jodi said, pulling up her legs and sitting Indian-style. "Hit me."

Zack smiled. "What countries border Pakistan?" he asked.

Jodi blinked and was immediately embarrassed. She should definitely know this. "Uh . . . Afghanistan?"

"Right . . . ," he said. "There are three more."

"What?!" Jodi exclaimed. Zack's smile turned triumphant. "Okay, I have no idea," she added. Her heart was pounding so hard, she was sure it could be heard throughout the deserted library.

"China, India, and Iran," Zack said.

Jodi rolled her eyes. She could have at least gotten India. Duh.

"You have to kiss me . . . here," Zack said, pointing to the spot just below his chin but not quite on his neck. One of Jodi's favorite spots to be kissed.

She leaned forward, bracing her hands on the floor, and gave him a long, slow kiss. When she pulled back again, Zack's eyes were closed and she had already managed to turn herself on.

She breathed deeply. "My turn," she said. "Name one professional soccer team."

Zack opened his mouth, and a little squeaking sound came out. His face fell, and he snapped his mouth shut again. "The Spurs?" he said.

Jodi made an obnoxious buzzing sound. "They're basketball. Nice try." She scooted closer to him and turned her head. "You have to kiss me here," she said, pointing to her earlobe.

A chill skittered over her skin as Zack leaned in and ever so slowly kissed the tip of her ear. And kept kissing it. Until she almost melted into his arms.

"My turn!" Zack announced, startling her out of the fantasy that was taking shape in her mind. She and Zack, completely naked, rolling around on the library floor.

Forget it. There was no way she could answer quiz questions right now. "Oh, no, you don't," she said. Her eyelids heavy, she turned to Zack, wrapped her hand around the back of his neck and pulled him to her. This time Zack kissed her back. Enthusiastically.

Before Jodi knew it, they *were* rolling around on the library floor, albeit fully clothed. They made out for what felt like hours until finally, exhausted, they both lay on their backs between piles of books.

"Wow," Zack said.

"I second that," Jodi replied happily.

"We should really shelve these books," he said with a huge yawn.

"Uh-huh," she said, feeling quite groggy herself. She turned on her side and cuddled into the crook of Zack's arm, a perfect fit. Closing her eyes, she murmured, "In a minute."

When Jodi opened her eyes again, bright sunlight was streaming through the enormous library windows.

"Omigod!" she exclaimed, sitting up. "Zack!"

She shoved his shoulder, and he started awake. "Wha?"

"We have to get out of here!" Jodi said, glancing at her watch. "The library opens in fifteen minutes. Hank is going to fire our asses."

Zack jumped to his feet. He and Jodi raced for the lobby, straightening their hair and clothes as they went. When they were safely outside, Jodi struggled for breath and looked at Zack.

"Your face is all creased on one side," she said with a smirk.

"Your hair is sticking up like half a mohawk," he shot back.

Jodi reached up to try to pat it down. "So . . . I guess I'll see you," she said, wishing they had five minutes to figure out what all that kissing *meant*.

"Yeah," Zack said with a lopsided smile. "Definitely."

Jodi turned and, swinging her bag at her side, headed for Maize Hall. At least she had gotten a *definitely*.

22

Later that day Ali stood in the outer office at Rocco Lee's, barely able to contain her excitement. She'd been invited over to watch an investors-only screening of the dailies from the movie Rocco was making with the help of her money. It was just so chic. So Hollywood. She was a film producer! Ali couldn't wait to see what the rest of the investors looked like. Maybe one of them would be semifamous!

Unfortunately, she was unfashionably early. No one else had arrived yet.

"Alison! You're here, good!" Rocco Lee said, opening the door to his little office. "I had to get rid of my secretary, so I don't know what the hell is going on half the time."

Ali laughed. "That's okay."

"Well, come on in," Rocco said. He scratched at the exposed patch of neck hair peeking out of the top of his shirt.

"Uh . . . aren't we going to a screening room or something?" Ali asked. She'd been envisioning a mini-movie theater with high-tech equipment like the one she'd seen on one of the many episodes of *Cribs* she'd watched over the summer.

"Nah. You have any idea how much those places cost?" Rocco said with a snort.

Her smile faltering, Ali stepped into Rocco's office. There were two chairs set up in front of a small flickering TV screen. Rocco hit the lights and Ali's danger radar went off. Where were the rest of the investors? Was she really going to sit alone in the dark with Rocco Lee?

Don't be a loser, she told herself. *You're a movie producer. Act professional!*

Ali lowered herself into the chair on the left. Rocco popped a video tape into the VCR and sat down next to her. His bulky frame took up the chair and then some, and his arm brushed hers. Ali moved her knees so that they were pointing away from Rocco.

"Here goes," he said, making a popping sound with his tongue.

Suddenly the screen was filled with a huge, white ass. Ali immediately thought of Mooner, but the next second all she could see was her future flashing before her eyes. The guy with the butt was getting it on with no fewer than three women, right there on the mini-TV in Rocco Lee's office. Ali felt her stomach turn, and she started to sweat.

"What the hell is this?" she said. There was moaning. Lots of moaning.

"It's called *Ballin' Rouge*—get it?" Rocco Lee said, delighted. "It's a take off on *Moulin Rouge*."

Ali stood up and turned on the lights. "It's a porno? You used my money to make a porno?"

Rocco Lee stood as well, shoving his hands into the pockets of his sharkskin suit. "Actually, I was wondering if you might consider making another investment," he said as the moaning and groaning on the TV grew louder. "See, I kind of took your three g's to one of those riverboat casinos and—"

"You *lost* my money?" Ali screeched. Suddenly she knew she was going to faint. She'd never fainted before, but she knew. She reached out for the wall and steadied herself.

"Hey, baby, chill," Rocco Lee said, approaching her with a less than savory look in his pouchy eyes. "If you can't make another investment, there are other ways you can help out with the film."

Ali watched his hand coming toward her chest with a sort of detached wonder. This could not be happening. She had not just lost half of her tuition money to a sleazeball porn king.

Before Ali even knew what she was doing, she'd pulled back her leg and kneed Rocco Lee right in his groin. He doubled over and hit the floor just as one of the women on the screen was screaming "Yes!" at the top of her lungs.

Ali reached over, hit eject, and grabbed the videotape. If he'd lost her money, she was going to lose something of his. Without a second look back, she fled the dingy little office.

Her first instinct was to run right home and sob all over

her roommates, but she knew that Jodi and Celeste both had classes this afternoon. When Ali came around a corner and saw Dimers, PU's campus dive bar, she almost cried with relief. A drink. She could definitely use a drink right now.

Three thousand dollars, Ali thought, still clutching the tape as she lowered herself onto a bar stool. *Three thousand dollars up in smoke!* She had only twenty-eight hundred left. That wasn't enough to keep her in school. How could she have proved her father right? How could she have messed up so badly?

"Beer," Ali said to the bartender, wiping a tear from her cheek with the back of her hand.

A guy with shaggy brown hair and a T-shirt with the sleeves ripped off sat down on the stool next to hers. He smelled like a mixture of Tide and onion rings. He had a cool electric guitar tattoo on his outer arm—red with a little yellow bolt of lightning on it.

"Tattoos," Ali muttered. "Maybe I'll be a tattoo artist."

"You like tattoos?" the guy asked. Ali looked up at his face for the first time. He had gorgeous green eyes and a chiseled-yet-sweet look about him. Like that lead singer of the Goo Goo Dolls.

"Whatever," she said with a shrug. She stuffed the video into her bag as the bartender slapped a beer in front of her.

"I'm Mark," the tattoo guy said.

Too bad I already have my M, Ali thought.

Then she thought of her lost money again and almost

hurled. Three thousand dollars. She'd just lost three thousand dollars and the AHUL was still the first thing on her mind. What kind of person was she?

Her stomach lurched violently, and Ali heaved herself off her chair, rushing for the bathroom. After she splashed some cold water on her face, she took the videotape out of her bag, set it down on the floor, lifted her boot, and smashed it with every ounce of strength in her body. Goodbye, movie career, hello, poverty.

Goodbye, college.

Ali opened the door and returned to the bar. She noticed a few of her girls from the Lesbian Alliance at a booth and walked over to join them. It was time to get plastered.

23

Jodi went to work that afternoon, her heart pounding nervously. She still had no idea what last night had meant to Zack. All she knew was that it had been incredible and she'd kill to do it again. Was it even remotely possible that he felt the same way?

Well, you're about to get your answer, Jodi thought, the moment she saw Zack shelving books on the third floor. Just the sight of him made her skin tingle.

Jodi was about to walk up to him, but she couldn't do it. She had no idea what to say. Instead she grabbed a pile of books and started shelving just down the row from him. Let him come to her. A much better plan.

Out of the corner of her eye she saw him move. He was coming toward her. Jodi steeled herself.

"Hey," Zack said, moving past her.

"Hey," Jodi replied. She felt a little breathless.

Then he disappeared down the next row. Jodi's arms dropped. What the hell was *that?* When had she ever known Zack not to be wordy?

Suddenly the giddy what's-going-to-happen? feeling was gone, leaving a heavy lump of disappointment in its place. Jodi placed a few more books on the shelves, her face starting to heat up. Where did he get off with his little "hey"? You didn't just have a totally amazing all-night make-out session with a person and then say, "Hey."

Jodi dropped the rest of her books and headed for Zack's row. She was going to force him to talk to her. There was no way she was going to make it through the rest of the shift feeling like this.

She came around the corner and Zack looked up. Their eyes met for a split second, and Jodi thought she saw an apology in his face. Her heart lightened briefly, but then he looked away.

"Uh, Jodi?" a voice said from behind her. She turned around to find Hank of the practically nonexistent goatee standing there. "We need to talk."

Jodi cast one last look at Zack, who was watching her and Hank, clearly alarmed. Then she followed Hank back to his office. Jodi couldn't get her thoughts straight. Why was Zack so freaked when he saw Hank talking to her? Was he jealous or something? Well, at least *that* would be a good sign.

"We're going to have to let you go," Hank said the moment she was through the door of the office.

Jodi's heart dropped. "What! Why?" she asked.

"Well, without getting into the sordid details, let's just say we have videotape of you and some guy sneaking out of the library this morning looking all disheveled," Hank said flatly. "That is not Allween Library behavior."

Jodi was speechless. *Me and some guy?* So they hadn't recognized Zack on the tape.

"So you're out," Hank said. "And it would be good if you'd tell me who the guy was because if it's someone who works here, he's out, too."

Jodi opened her mouth with Zack's name right on the tip of her tongue. It would be so great to get back at him for that little "hey" episode upstairs. But she couldn't do it. However angry she was, she didn't want him to lose his job.

"I never kiss and tell. Well, Hank, it's been real," Jodi said. Then she turned on her heel and stalked out, leaving Hank, her job, and Zack behind.

24

The next day, Celeste sat in music humanities, dying for the lecture to end for three equally disturbing reasons:

1. Professor McKean was wearing a wedding band. He was married. Which made her not only a false slut, but a false adulterous slut.

2. She could feel Carter's eyes boring into the back of her head from the rear of the classroom and she did not want to deal with him.

3. Eve the Lesbian Alliance girl was staring her down as well.

Was Eve hitting on her? Right there in class? *Eeew.* Celeste had told the girl she was straight. And from the way Eve had freaked the last time they talked, Celeste also thought she hated her.

When the class finally ended, Celeste grabbed her things as fast as she could and practically ran out of the room. But the moment she was through the door, she bumped right into someone who had come out the door at the back of the room.

Don't let it be Carter, Celeste thought, staring at her feet.

"Sorry," the guy said.

Not Carter's voice. Celeste looked up into deep green eyes behind wire-rimmed glasses. She had noticed this guy before. He had a sort of classic look, like someone you might see wearing a toga on a tapestry in the Cloisters. Except that none of the Cloisters guys had red-and-yellow guitar tattoos.

"Hey," he said.

"Hi," Celeste said, frozen.

Even though he hadn't said more than "hey," he was really saying it in a very *interested* way. Despite everything she had on her mind, like the fact that she had forced an unsuspecting victim to commit imaginary adultery, she felt extremely open to that "hey."

"My name's David," he said, lifting one corner of his mouth in a sexy smile.

"Hey, *David,*" she said. David. What a nice name. It was her favorite uncle's name. It was the name of her favorite statue in Florence.

Best of all, it started with *D.*

If she could just secretly redo the letters she had lied about, she would be on *D* right now. Maybe, just for the sake of her conscience, she would keep trying—go back and do the AHUL for real. Especially if she could start with David.

"So . . . do you like this class?" he asked.

"Yeah, it's okay," Celeste said. *And getting better every minute,* she thought. If only she could think of a reason to kiss this guy.

Then the back door to the classroom opened and Carter walked out. The moment he saw her, he started toward her with that lazy smile of his. The last thing she wanted to do was talk to Carter Mann.

And so she did the one thing that might turn the geriatric pot-smoker around. She grabbed classic-looking David and she kissed him. He didn't even seem surprised. He kissed her so deeply, she felt it in her toes.

Breathless, Celeste finally broke away from David, and Carter was gone. She looked up at David's green eyes and giggled. She couldn't help it. And once she started, there was no stopping her.

"Thanks!" she said through her laughing fit. Then she turned and ran all the way back to Maize Hall, feeling quite proud of the limb she'd just walked out on. Unfortunately, she couldn't share her triumph with Ali and Jodi. After all, they thought she was *way* past *D*.

25

Ali rushed toward room 213 with a long loaf of French bread sticking out of her backpack and burst into the triple. Jodi and Celeste were moping on their beds.

"Dudes!" Ali said.

Jodi and Celeste barely looked up.

"I have a surprise for you," Ali said.

No one said anything.

"Hey, what's wrong with you guys?" Ali asked.

"Nothing," Jodi mumbled.

"Well, maybe this will cheer you up," Ali said. "We're going to Paris."

Jodi and Celeste exchanged blank looks.

Ali pulled three airplane tickets out of her bag, along with the baguette and a small wheel of Brie. "We're going to Paris!" she said again. She handed Celeste and Jodi their tickets. "I just hope you dudes have passports."

Jodi and Celeste looked down in disbelief at their names typed out on the tickets. This didn't seem like a joke. They were holding real round-trip tickets to Charles de Gaulle Airport.

"What is this?" Jodi asked.

"It's my gift to you guys," Ali said. She looked as excited as a little kid on Christmas morning, but she was the one giving presents.

"But how much did these cost?" Celeste asked. It was like a million dollars to go to Paris.

"Never mind about that," Ali said. "Like I said, they are a *gift*. Anyway, you can thank my father. He sent me some extra money when he found out my grades were getting so much better. I know how bummed out everyone's been for the last couple of days and besides, we have the long Veterans Day weekend right around the corner and—"

"Ali . . . we can't accept these," Celeste said. "This is your money. You should do something for yourself with it."

"Yeah," Jodi said, handing the ticket back even though it almost caused her physical pain. She'd *always* wanted to go to Paris. "We can't let you spend all that money on us."

"You're not *letting* me do anything!" Ali proclaimed, handing the ticket right back. "We're going, and that's final! Besides, it will help me to immerse myself in ze French culture," she said with a bad French accent. "I can do an extra-credit report for Schwartz and get him off my back!"

Ali was getting so good at lying, she almost believed herself. She watched Celeste and Jodi exchange a look and knew she had them. She smiled wistfully. Little did they know that this little jaunt over the pond was going to be the last time they'd ever hang out together. Ali had used the last of her funds on the tickets. There was no point in saving it when it wouldn't cover her tuition, anyway.

Instead, she'd decided it was time to live a little. Especially since her dad would be killing her soon.

"So . . . we're actually going to Paris?" Jodi asked, looking her ticket over again—holding it gingerly.

"That's right!" Ali said.

Celeste burst out laughing as Jodi screamed and jumped up and down like a lunatic.

Ali broke a piece off the baguette. "*La baguette*, anyone?"

"No way," Jodi said. "From now on I'm staying completely off carbs. Do you have any idea how skinny the girls are in France?"

"So does that mean you accept?" Ali asked. It hadn't really occurred to her that they would say no, but now that they almost had, she realized it had been kind of risky buying three nonrefundable tickets without asking them first.

"Yes!" Celeste and Jodi said in unison. The three girls hugged. *Vive la France!*

26

On Thursday night Jodi, Celeste, and Ali, along with enough luggage to sink a ship, boarded Air France flight 213[20] to Paris, France. When they deboarded, two in-flight movies later, they were all seriously hung over from all the free champagne.

But they were there. In Paris!

"Dude, what are we going to do now that we're here?" Ali asked.

"Kiss lots of boys," Celeste said, slipping her sunglasses over her eyes.

"Paris is supposed to be very romantic," Jodi said with a shrug. She didn't mention that the only boy she was interested in kissing at all was a guy named Zack who had blown her off. And who wasn't in Paris.

They dragged themselves off the plane and Ali stopped at a foreign currency exchange booth to get some euros. She

□□□□□□□□□□□□□□□□□□□□□□□□□□□□□□□

20 The flight number was the same as their room number, which they took to be a good omen.

handed the woman one hundred dollars and got back a bit more than a hundred euros.

"We're rich!" Ali said, examining the bills. "Let's get a cab!"

They climbed into a waiting taxi outside the airport and gave the driver the name of their hotel, then sat back to take in the sights. It took Jodi only about ten minutes to realize that everything she'd heard about the romance of Paris was true. Everywhere she looked, people were kissing. They kissed at bus stops and on buses, at cafés and on street corners. One couple kissed and rode their bikes at the same time.

"Wow, you guys! Just look!" Celeste said, pointing out the window. They were stopped on one of the many quaint bridges that crossed the Seine, and one of the Bateaux Mouches—boats touring Paris along the river Seine—was just passing beneath them. But that wasn't what had Celeste frozen in awe. She was looking up at the spires of Notre-Dame. The actual Notre-Dame cathedral. She could barely breathe, it was so beautiful.

"No, look at *that*," Ali said, pointing out the other window. They could just see the top of the Eiffel Tower in the distance. "If that monster phallic symbol doesn't get you in the mood for love, nothing will."

"Ali!" Celeste said, leaning over Jodi to whack her shoulder. But she couldn't help laughing as well. If someone had told her two months ago that she'd be sitting in a cab in Paris with the two best friends she'd ever had, she would have told them to have a little more of Jib's psychedelic pot and stop talking crazy.

Finally the cab driver pulled up in front of an old, run-down building on a cobblestone street.

"Voilà," he said. "You are 'ere."

Ali looked out the window at their temporary abode. The Hôtel Merci wasn't much to look at on the outside, but she was determined to be positive. She paid the driver and clambered out of the car with her friends.

"We'll get the bags," Jodi said.

Ali pulled the handle on the front door of the hotel, but the door was locked. Who ever heard of a hotel having a locked door? Jodi rang the doorbell, and after a while a man answered it. He was wearing nothing but boxer shorts and was yawning and rubbing his eyes like the girls had woken him. The hotel lobby was tiny. It had a small desk, a black-and-white television, and a small couch with a pillow and a blanket on it where the manager had obviously been sleeping.

"We have a reservation," Ali said. "Alison Sheppard."

The man scratched at his crotch and handed them one room key. "Wonder what *his* name is," Jodi said sarcastically under her breath.

The girls crowded themselves and their stuff into the tiniest elevator any of them had ever seen. When they opened the door to their room a few minutes later, they were hit with the smell of vanilla and roses. It smelled like one hundred years of built-up air freshener.

Jodi held her nose. "They should call this the Hotel Mercy," she said. But the view was amazing—just rooftops and chimneys. *C'est magnifique!*

They were going to shower but decided not to when they realized the shower was in the hall of the floor below them.

"Maybe we should take naps," Celeste suggested.

"I'm too excited to sleep," Jodi said.

"Let's go party," Ali suggested.

Celeste rallied and they left the hotel, whispering so they wouldn't wake up the manager again, and walked out into the most beautiful neighborhood they had ever seen.

"This place is unbelievable," Celeste said, actually executing a little twirl of happiness right in the middle of the street.

"Yeah, it is," Jodi said. *I wish Zack were here,* she added silently. If he were, she would kiss him in every one of the places they had passed in the cab—that is, if the two of them could just get past "hey."

27

The Hôtel Merci was on the Left Bank, near Montparnasse, where there were wine bars on every corner. Ali was feeling ready to party, but it was a little too early for Chardonnay. Instead they decided to do what they had really come to Paris to do.

See great art? No.

Dine on fine French cuisine? Nuh-uh.

Visits the famous cathedrals—Sacré Coeur and Notre-Dame? Well, Celeste was down with that, but there was no way she was going to convince her friends.

What they had come to do was shop, preferably for funny souvenirs and also some cool affordable clothes and jewelry so that when they were complimented on them, they could say, "Oh, *this?* I got this in *Paris.*"

The first place they went was the rue de Rivoli, near the Louvre, where there were all kinds of souvenir stands.

Ali bought them each a set of tiny Guerlain perfumes. Then Celeste found a perfume she loved. She sprayed the tester all over herself. It was called Pour les Chiens and it smelled delicious. Ali and Jodi agreed it was the nicest scent there and sprayed it on their pulse points, their wrists, and their cleavage. The salesgirl sneered at them.

"Why is she looking at us like that?" Celeste whispered.

"I have no idea," Ali said. "Dude, what's your damage?"

The woman simply smiled at them and said, *"Vous êtes les chiens?"*

Flustered and clueless, Celeste just smiled back. "Uh . . . *oui*," she said. *"Merci."* Then she grabbed Ali and Jodi by their arms and scurried off.

"What did that woman say to us?" Ali asked, pulling out her French-to-English dictionary as they walked. "Do they all have to talk so fast?"

"If you figure it out, let us know," Celeste replied.

"Where are we going, anyway?" Jodi asked once they were back on the street.

"My parents said we have to go to a place called Angelina, and it's supposed to be right near here," Celeste explained.

They walked along the rue de Rivoli until they found Angelina. It was an enormous fancy restaurant packed with people drinking tea and coffee and eating pastries. Their dogs were there, too, right in the restaurant. Some people even let their dogs sit at the table with them. They lapped water out of teacups and gobbled gooey pastries. No one seemed to think this was at all unusual.

Angelina's specialty was the *chocolat Africain*, which was a giant pitcher of the thickest hot chocolate you could ever imagine with a silver boat filled with whipped cream on the side. Jodi, Ali, and Celeste sat at a small round table and each ordered the *chocolat Africain.* They poured it into the pretty green-and-white cups and sipped it delicately. It was the most delicious thing they had ever tasted.

Celeste and Jodi pored over their guidebook as Ali continued to consult the dictionary, not even caring if they looked like tourists.

"Look," Ali said, pointing at a woman a few tables away from them. She was slumped over sound asleep in her chair. Ali flipped to another page in the dictionary, trying to find the word for narcoleptic. "*C'est les yeux paresseux* K.J. Martin . . . *narcoleptique!*" she improvised.

Jodi and Celeste both laughed. At least *they* understood her.

"There's something I want to say," Celeste said.

"What?" Jodi asked.

"I just want to say that this is absolutely the coolest thing I have ever done and I just really want to thank you guys because I think you're the coolest people I have ever known."

"I'll never forget this trip," Jodi said. "No matter what happens in my life, I will always remember the time we picked up and came to Paris."

Ali just sat there beaming. It was worth the money. It was worth everything. She was a million miles away from her problems and having the time of her life.

The check came, and Ali paid the whole thing even though Jodi and Celeste protested. Each *chocolat Africain* was eight euros and worth every bit.

"What should we do now?" Celeste asked.

But before they could answer, a big white poodle trotted over to them and began sniffing under their table. Ali felt it push its wet nose up against her wrist before it moved on to Celeste.

"What the—" Ali said.

The dog had an enormous erection. It put its two front legs up on Celeste's lap and started licking her face.

"Whoa, there, dog," Celeste said, trying to fend the thing off.

"I heard French men were like this, but I didn't know French dogs were, too," Jodi said, trying not to laugh. The whole thing was a little too disturbing for laughter.

Celeste, meanwhile, was far from happy. This beast was really getting fresh.

"It's your first sexual experience since Buster," Ali said.

"Yeah, and they're both dogs!" Jodi piped in.

"Omigod! I just realized what that bitch back there said to us!" Ali exclaimed. "She asked if we were dogs! And that's what *Pour les Chiens* means! 'For the dogs!'"

"Are you telling me I'm covered in *dog* perfume?" Celeste shrieked.

Jodi couldn't help it. She cracked up.

"Get this thing off me!" Celeste said. The poodle was licking her whole face with his big pink tongue.

Ali grabbed the dog and pulled him away from Celeste. A tall, flustered lady came over and clipped a leash to the poodle's collar.

"*Je m'excuse! Je m'excuse!*" she said apologetically before leading the horny dog away.

"I have to go wash up," Celeste said, grimacing as she stood. "What were they thinking putting dog perfume next to real perfume?"

"What were they thinking *manufacturing* dog perfume?" Jodi asked.

"They were thinking they really love their dogs," Ali put in.

They all ran upstairs to the fancy bathroom, and Celeste hit the sink to wash off the dog drool.

"Hey," Jodi said as she went into a bathroom stall and closed the door. "Have you noticed how small the toilet paper is here? Why is the toilet paper so skinny? It's about half the width of ours."

"Have you seen the girls here?" Ali asked. "They have the smallest asses in the world. Their asses are half as big as ours."

Maybe it was from lack of sleep or maybe it was from practically being raped by a poodle, but for some reason, Celeste thought that was the funniest thing she had ever heard. She cracked up, and soon Jodi and Ali were laughing with her.

"You guys want to go down and buy some Angelina souvenirs?" Ali asked, wiping tears of mirth from her eyes.

"I'm getting my souvenir right here," Celeste said. She grabbed an extra roll of toilet paper and stuffed it in her bag. She had a feeling this was a moment she'd never want to forget, poodle and all.

28

"Well, should we go in?" Jodi asked, as they stood facing the entrance to the Louvre. It was the biggest museum any of them had ever seen.

"Maybe we should just dash in, take one quick look at the *Mona Lisa*, and split," Ali said.

"I don't know," Jodi said. "I mean, it costs money to go in, and we really should be responsible with our money."

Celeste vehemently agreed.

"That's true," Ali said. "I mean, there are so many cute little wine bars right around our hotel, and we still want to buy things. We really shouldn't waste the money on the museum."

And so, *purely* for economic reasons, they skipped the Louvre and hopped in a cab.

"Eiffel Tower, *s'il vous plaît*," Ali said, then shot a triumphant look at Celeste and Jodi. Her French classes were paying off after all!

They took the elevator to the top of the tower and stood on the observation deck, looking out at all of Paris.

"I want to do that," Jodi said, pointing to the biggest Ferris wheel she had ever seen.

"I want to do *that*!" Ali said, looking through a telescope machine at something on the ground.

"What?" Jodi and Celeste asked. They couldn't see anything. Finally Ali let them take a look. She had the telescope trained on a man—a French police officer man.

"That's what you're looking at? That cop?" Celeste said.

"Isn't he the most gorgeous thing you have ever seen in your entire life?" Ali said dreamily. "That's it—I'm definitely moving here. And I'm kissing him; I don't care what his name is."

"You can't kiss a cop," Celeste said.

"Why not? You kissed a teacher," Ali reminded her. Celeste wished she hadn't, even though she hadn't.

Ali headed for the elevator, Jodi and Celeste at her heels, and waited impatiently. When it finally reached the ground, she practically pushed other tourists out of the way to get to her cop.

"Bonjour," she said, when she caught up with him.

"Bonjour," he said, barely looking at her.

"Je suis de les Etats-Unis," Ali said. It had sounded kind of cool in her head when she said it but, it sounded unbelievably stupid when the words came out of her mouth.

The cop just nodded slightly and looked right past her. He had the most incredible blue eyes she had ever seen and the blackest hair and the deepest cleft in his perfectly sculpted chin. She couldn't decide if he was the French George

Clooney or the French Tom Cruise. She had to kiss him. She just had to. So she did.

She stood on her toes and touched her lips to his. For a moment he was as cold as stone, and then suddenly he was kissing her back. It was amazing. Or as the French say, *magnifique!*

Suddenly he pulled away and cleared his throat nervously. Clearly, he was not supposed to be kissing tourists. But just as clearly, he'd enjoyed it.

"Let's get out of here!" Jodi said, pulling on Ali's arm. Another cop was approaching, and he looked none too pleased with his partner.

"Merci!" Ali called out, waving frantically as she was pulled away.

Ali, Celeste, and Jodi jogged across the square and up the steps to the road above, laughing the whole way.

"Did you see that cop's face when he pulled away?" Celeste said when they stopped for breath. "He was totally in love!"

Ali just grinned, starry-eyed.

"All I know is, we have to get a camera. I mean, *that* was a Kodak moment," Jodi said.

29

"Dude, let's go to McDonald's," Ali said, pointing at a huge, three-story Mickey-D's on the Champs-Elysées.

Celeste scrunched her nose. She couldn't believe the people of Paris had let the famous roadway be tarnished by a McDonald's.

"I did not come all the way to Paris to eat a Big Mac," Celeste said. "Let's go in here."

She opened the door to a quaint-looking brasserie, where they all ended up ordering *croque monsieurs*. It was a thoroughly enjoyable culinary experience—until they noticed a cockroach crawling on the wall.

They ditched their sandwiches and headed down the street to have their portrait painted by a street vendor. It was worth it just to have a chance to sit down and rest their aching feet.[21] The artist agreed to do them all together instead of individually, and when it was done,

□□□□□□□□□□□□□□□□□□□□□□□□□□□□□

21 Cobblestones kill!

they wished they had two more copies. The portrait was beautiful, but Celeste loved it even more than her friends did. The artist had given her very long eyelashes for some reason.

"This is on me," Ali said, handing the artist twenty euros.

"No!" Jodi said. "You've been paying for everything. This is crazy."

"We're paying for the whole rest of the trip," Celeste said.

But again, Ali absolutely insisted on paying. The artist had signed the portrait Nero.

"Check it out, guys," she said, pointing to the signature. "I'm on *N*."

"Be our guest," Jodi said shook her head slightly. Ali really was a kissing machine.

"*Merci*, dude," Ali said to Nero.

"What iz zis 'dude'?" Nero asked.

It was so sweet that she kissed him right then and got paint on her cheek.

"*Non, sank you,*" Nero said. "*J'adore les jeunes filles des Etats-Unis! J'adore zis* 'dude.'"

Ali blew him another kiss, and the girls headed off to one of the docking stations for the Bateaux Mouches. It was amazing to float down the river and look at the city, the lovers on the banks, the beautiful centuries-old buildings, the opera house, the spires of Notre-Dame.

As Jodi slouched back in her seat, taking it all in, she noticed a cute man leaning against the railing of the boat, taking pictures.

"He's like the French Leonardo DiCaprio and this is like the French *Titanic*," Jodi said.

The man noticed her noticing him and said something to them in French. Jodi looked at her friends, but it was clear they had no idea what he was saying, so they all just started giggling.

"Ah, American?" he asked.

They nodded.

He held up his camera. "I ask you if I may make your photograph?"

"Okay," Ali said.

He took their pictures with all of Paris as the backdrop.

"I love to make the photographs of the beautiful women," he said, tucking his long blond bangs behind his ear.

Jodi, Ali, and Celeste nearly swooned. What was better than this? While he changed rolls of film, they huddled together for a hushed conference.

"Who gets to kiss him?" Jodi asked. This guy could probably help her forget all about mean old grumpy Zack.

"How about we ask him his name, and whoever's next letter is closest to his name gets to kiss him?" Celeste suggested.

"Who's going to ask him?" Jodi asked.

"I will," Celeste said boldly.

She walked up to him and said, *"Excuse moi. Comment t'appelle tu?"*

"My name is Alain, but everybody, zay call me Kiev," he

said. "It is, how you say, nickyname, because I am as juicy, as, how you say, tasty, as a shit-ken Kiev."

"You mean chicken Kiev,"[22] Celeste coached. *"Excuse moi,"* she said, and joined her friends a few feet away. "He says his name is Kiev."

"I'm on *K*!" Jodi said. "I win. I sooo win."

Celeste and Ali stayed behind while Jodi approached Kiev.

"I'd love to see your photographs some time," she said.

"You will give me your address and I will send you, no? And we will, how you say, touch each other," Kiev suggested politely.

Well, that was an invitation if Jodi had ever heard one. She leaned in and her lips touched his. After a moment of surprise, Kiev kissed her back so delicately, she almost lost her balance. When she finally pulled away, they were both smiling.

"I should tell you somezing," Kiev said quietly.

"Yes?" Jodi replied, floating.

"I am sorry, but I am gay, *ma chere amie*," he said.

Jodi blinked. "Wow," she said. "Then you are going to make some lucky guy *very* happy."

Kiev beamed.

The boat began to dock and Ali and Celeste moved toward the exit.

"Well, thanks for the kiss," Jodi said to Kiev as he gathered his things. She turned to catch up with her friends.

___

22 Chicken dish invented in Kiev in which chicken is rolled with butter and herbs.

"Wait!" Kiev said, following them off the boat. "You don't give me your address!"

"Oh, right!" Jodi said. Kiev handed her a scrap of paper and a pen from his camera bag and she scribbled down her Pollard PO box and handed it back to him. "Thanks again!"

They watched Kiev scurry off through the crowd, and then Ali turned to Jodi with a smile. "Wow! He wants your address?" Ali said, impressed. "That must have been some kiss."

"It's not like he's going to come visit. He just wants to send us our picture," Jodi said, lifting one shoulder. "Besides, he's gay."

Ali and Celeste followed Jodi down the street. "You're kidding. Wait, but didn't he kiss you back?" Celeste asked. "We were watching from across the boat. It sure looked like he was into it."

"What can I say?" Jodi said, walking backwards so she could see them. She lifted her arms nonchalantly. "I am just that irresistible."

They all dissolved into a giggling fit and headed for the hotel.

30

On their last night in Paris, Jodi, Ali, and Celeste decided to ride the giant Ferris wheel. But at the last minute Celeste chickened out and stayed on the ground while Jodi and Ali took a ride.

Celeste was standing happily on terra firma, looking up at the massive wheel, when she was startled by a man who had come up behind her. "Are you afraid?" he asked.

Celeste had been trying to act French all weekend, so she was disappointed to be spoken to in English.

"How did you know I speak English?" she asked.

"I am psychic," he said. He had a French accent, but his English was excellent. "No, actually, I was behind you and your friends when you bought your tickets. Why did you choose to stay behind?"

"Last minute jitters," Celeste said.

He cocked his head quizzically. "I don't know what jitters are, but you seem to me to be the adventurous type."

Celeste was flattered. *Beaucoup* flattered.

"Shall we go up together?" he asked.

What the hell? She *was* the adventurous type, after all. *"Oui!"* Celeste said. She waved to Jodi and Ali as their cage came around and pointed to the man next to her and then up at the ride. She hoped they would understand she was going on the ride and to wait for her.

The man produced two tickets from his pocket, and they boarded the ride together. They sat across from each other, and Celeste was a little nervous to discover just how much the cage swayed back and forth. This thing was way bigger than any Ferris wheel she had seen at Coney Island. And it was truly dizzying to reach the top, swaying back and forth like that, and see the Eiffel Tower, the Seine, the Arc de Triomphe, everything.

"It's so beautiful up here," Celeste said. "What's your name?"

"My name is Jacques," he said. "And what is yours?"

In a way, Jacques was like the French Carter. He was handsome and sexy in a Carter kind of way, but he looked younger. He had choppy blond hair and blue eyes and an earring in his left ear.

"I'm Celeste," she replied. "Um—how old are you?" It was an awkward question, but considering what she'd been through, she had to find out.

"I am twenty-four," he said, smiling.

Great, Celeste thought. He was a normal age. And wait a minute. She was up to *J* on her fake list—the one she had made up in the bathroom. She was really only up to *E*, but as far as her friends knew, it was *J.* Jacques. Absolutely. *Absolument.*

"It is a wonderful view," Jacques said. But he wasn't looking out at Paris; his eyes were glued to her face.

Celeste blushed.

"You are very beautiful, but I am sure you are told this often," he said.

Celeste felt her skin color deepen to what had to be a dark purple. She was grateful that it was night and that everything was obscured by the blinking lights of the Ferris wheel.

"Thank you," she said after taking a moment to absorb the fact that someone had just called her beautiful. "Uh, *merci.*"

"You speak French well," he said. "You are easy to communicate with."

The Ferris wheel had stopped, suspending them all the way on top in midair, but to Celeste, it might as well have been still spinning. Could there be a more perfect, romantic moment?

"Are you still scared?"

"Yes, a little," Celeste admitted. But she was more swooning than scared.

"Let me help you," Jacques said. He carefully shifted over to her side of the cage, sitting on the bench next to her. Then he put his arm around her. "Better?"

"Yes," Celeste said, even though when he had made the seat change, the car had dipped dramatically and so had her stomach.

"Do you think I could kiss you?" Jacques asked. "I am finding it difficult to resist you. Maybe it is your eyes, or your mouth, or that seductive scent you are wearing."

Celeste closed her eyes, and Jacques kissed her softly and then passionately. The cage went around and around, and they didn't stop kissing. He kissed her ears and eyes and lips. He coaxed her up on his lap, and they kissed like that for a long time. Celeste could feel his excitement through his pants.

When the wheel stopped, the ride operator didn't even make them get out. He was used to it—this was Paris—and they went around and around again. Meanwhile Jodi and Ali stood on the ground, looking up at them in disbelief. Way to go, Celeste!

"I wish I could invite you back to my room," Celeste said, breathlessly, when the two finally broke apart for a moment. "But I'm sharing a room with friends."

"Oh, but I can go no further, I am afraid," Jacques said.

A guy who didn't want to go further? That was weird. "Why not?" Celeste asked.

He smiled. "I am married, *chérie*," he said.

"Oh," Celeste said, completely taken aback. Her stomach lurched again, but not because of the ride. "But you're not wearing a—"

"A ring? No, I hate them. You are not upset, I hope?" Jacques said. "You understand, there is nothing wrong with an innocent kiss? My wife and I agree."

"What? Oh, no, no," Celeste said, flustered.

Wife! She had to get off this ride. She was becoming a serial husband kisser! Well, the first one had been a lie, but still!

Finally the ride came to a stop and she got off, barely saying good-bye to Jacques. She was so upset, she started to cry the moment her feet hit the ground. She ran over to her friends.

"I need a double Chardonnay, pronto," she said.

Ali found them a bar, and after numerous Chardonnays had been consumed by all, Celeste told Jodi and Ali the whole story.

"He's married!" she cried. "I feel so disgusting. I feel so terrible for his wife. We were making out, you know, *really, really* making out, and he's married."

"So?" Ali asked with a hiccup.

"So!" Celeste said. Was the whole world crazy?

"I don't—hic—understand," Ali said. She must have been really drunk. She never hiccupped unless she was really drunk.

"Celeste," Jodi joined in, waving her half-empty glass of Chardonnay around and sloshing some over the side. "I think what Ali is saying is she doesn't see what the big deal is about Jacques being married because you kissed Professor McKean, right? And he has a wife."

Celeste froze. How did Ali and Jodi know he was married? They weren't in any of McKean's classes, and Celeste had definitely not discussed his marital status with them. "How did you know McKean is married?" Celeste asked nervously.

"Ali told me," Jodi said. She placed her glass on the edge of the table and it fell off and shattered. No one seemed to notice. She frowned at Ali. "How did you know, Ali?"

Ali squinted, hiccupping and trying to remember.

"I don't know how I know," she said. "Oh—hic—yes, I do. I got really drunk at Dimers the other night after barfing in the bathroom—hic. It wasn't exactly my finest moment—hic—but anyway, I saw some people I know and one of them was in your class—hic—and, I don't know, it just seemed like they knew you kissed the guy—hic—and they were all shocked, especially because McKean has a wife he's supposedly so in love with and especially since she's pregnant and everything."

Hiccup, hiccup, hiccup. Ali took a long slug of wine to clear her throat.

"Pregnant!" Celeste blurted. Her mind raced. Who were these people and how did they know about the fake kiss? Did Ali actually tell them and not remember telling them? Had they told anyone else?

Before she could discuss it further with Ali and Jodi, they were off being pawed by several guys at the bar and arguing about their lists.

"Dude, all their names start with J. We're already past J," Ali said, her hiccups now under control.

"So maybe we can use the second part of their names!" Jodi said. She grabbed the arm of the guy next to her and looked drunkenly up into his face. "What's your whole name?"

"I am Jean-Philippe Berlain," he said.

Jodi let go of him and turned back to Ali, while Jean-Philippe returned to his drink, confused.

"See! He could be a *P*!" Jodi said loudly. Ali's face kind of teetered before her.

"Yeah, but we're not up to *P*. This guy over here is Jean-Michel, so he could be an *M*, but you're only up to *L*," Ali said.

She turned around on her stool and nudged a guy with her foot. He looked at her, annoyed.

"Comment t'appelle vous?" Ali said, getting her pronouns mixed.

"'Onoré," he said with a bit of a sneer.

"Ah! An *O*!" Ali said. She stood up and gave him a big wet one right on the mouth. He slipped her the tongue pretty quickly for a guy who'd been shooting her a death glare two seconds ago.

"Um . . . hate to be the one to tell you this, but I think it's Honoré, with an *H*," Jodi said when Ali was done.

"You're kidding," Ali said, wiping her mouth.

"Wait! Kiss that guy at the end of the bar," Jodi said helpfully. "I think his name is Jean-Ormonde."

"Killer," Ali said. She slipped off her bar stool and maneuvered her way over to the dark-haired guy in question. She kissed him without so much as a hello, then fell over. Luckily Jean-Ormonde caught her.

"All right, that's it," Celeste said. At that moment, the pregnant wife of her professor seemed like a lesser concern than what her friends might be about to do. "This is getting a little out of control."

She got up, quickly apologized to the guys at the bar, and hustled her friends out to the street.

Finally they were all back safe in their hotel room—as safe as you can be breathing vanilla room freshener all night and having a strange man greeting you at the door in his boxer shorts.

"I can't believe we leave tomorrow," Jodi said. She and Celeste were lying on one of the double beds and Ali was on the other.

"I know. It feels like we got here five minutes ago, but at the same time it feels like we've been here for weeks," Celeste said.

"Let's see if Mr. Boxer Shorts dude will send up a bottle of champagne, my treat," Ali said. "I also wouldn't mind some *fromage* and crackers." She was obviously still inebriated, because this was not exactly the kind of hotel that had champagne.

Jodi and Celeste looked at each other. This was going too far. Why was Ali insisting on treating them to everything? It was crazy.

"Hey, Ali?" Jodi said gently.

"Yeah?"

"You know, Celeste and I were wondering if something's going on."

"What do you mean?" Ali asked, sounding totally defensive.

"It's nothing, really, it's just that you bought tickets for this amazing trip, which was so incredible of you, but then you just kept paying for everything," Celeste said. "And when we went to that restaurant, you ordered that gross foie gras stuff that was so expensive, and now you're talking about ordering champagne. . . ."

"And you wouldn't even let us treat you to anything, and that's not fair to you," Jodi continued.

"It just seems like something's up with you lately," Celeste said.

Ali sat up slowly, feeling slightly pissed off and put on the spot. Was this a fucking *intervention* or something? But the moment she saw her roommates' sincere, expectant faces, the whole story suddenly started pouring out of her. About how her father hadn't actually sent her more money for doing so well in school. Even though she'd been studying more, even though Celeste had offered to help her, she was actually about to flunk out—seriously *fail* two of her classes.

"There must be something we can do," Jodi said.

"You know I meant it when I offered to help," Celeste said. "I can help you write your next Intro to Feminist Thought paper."

"I can't stay in school now, anyway," Ali said morosely. "This is the worst part, you guys. I invested half my dad's money, you know, to make more and show him how responsible I was?"

Celeste had a bad feeling about this. "What did you invest in?" she asked.

"In a movie . . . that turned out to be a sleazy porn

movie," Ali admitted, looking at the floor. "And the sleazy porn guy took my money and lost it at craps or some shit."

"Omigod, Ali," Jodi said, sitting up straight.

"I didn't have enough left to pay the bursar, so I just spent the rest of the money on this trip," Ali finished with a sniffle.

"And when were you planning to tell us all this!?" Celeste asked, shocked.

"Well," Ali said sheepishly, "I wasn't."

"What!" Jodi cried.

"I was thinking of maybe cashing in my ticket back to Georgia and just staying here," Ali said.

Jodi and Celeste were flabbergasted. This was the last thing they'd expected.

"You've got to be kidding," Jodi said.

"We're not going to let you stay here!" Celeste shrieked.

Ali smiled. "You didn't let me finish. I was about to say that even though I *was* going to keep this whole thing a secret and just sort of disappear off the face of the earth, I've now decided that it wouldn't be fair to my roommates—my two best friends."

Celeste pushed herself off the bed and went over to give Ali a hug. "We're going to figure this out the second we get back to school," she said firmly.

"Absolutely," Jodi said, plopping down on Ali's other side and making it a group hug.

"Thanks," Ali said. "Now, let's get to sleep. I can't wait for the monster hangover I'm going to have in the morning."

31

In the morning Ali announced, through a massive headache, that they could not get on the airplane without visiting Jim Morrison's grave. It would be un-American and totally wrong. Jodi was up for the trek and since Celeste was less hung over than either of them, she couldn't argue with the plan. If they could do it, she could.

They were silent on the Métro ride there, each thinking over last night's revelation and wondering what she could do to keep Ali in school. Jodi would have logged more hours at the library if she hadn't been fired. Ali was wondering if she could get paid to be a test subject for medical experiments. Celeste was coming up blank.

By the time they got to Jim Morrison's graffiti- and flower-covered grave, they were all appropriately somber even though they were surrounded by happy, picture-clicking tourists.

"Wow. It's so beautiful," Jodi said, even though the place had obviously been trampled and trashed by fans. She watched the flickering candles on top of the headstone, mesmerized.

"The Doors forever! Whoooo!" a hot, shirtless guy with huge pecs shouted as he ran around the tiny yard.

"Shhh!" Celeste scolded him. "This is a grave site."

"Lighten up, baby," a leather-wearing biker guy said, slipping one arm around Celeste's shoulders and the other around Ali's. "Jim has moved on to a higher plane." He looked Ali up and down. "I could take *you* to a higher plane if you give me half an hour."

Ali rolled her eyes and scoffed. "We're trying to be reflective," she said, removing his solid arm from her shoulders. It didn't even occur to any of them to ask his name.

"So, what are we going to do?" Jodi asked as they moved away from the headstone so that a Chinese family could have their picture taken in front of it.

"I don't know," Celeste said. "I can get a job and give Ali the paycheck."

"I'm not going to let you do that," Ali said. "*I* should get a job, obviously."

"Okay, so you'll get a job," Jodi said. "That's something. And I'll find a new one, too. But that doesn't help much since most campus jobs pay crap and we need a big wad of cash, like, stat."

Celeste sighed and looked over her shoulder. "Is there any way we could steal Jim Morrison's gravestone and sell that?"

Ali laughed. "If I could steal Jim Morrison's tombstone, I'd want to keep it for myself."

"Why are you in such a good mood?" Jodi asked. "We have to get on a plane in an hour and go back to reality, which, by the way, sucks."

Ali looked from Jodi to Celeste and back again, thinking, *As long as I have them on my side, I'll be fine.* Of course, she'd never *say* anything that abominably cheesy.

"Nah," she said with a shrug. "Reality's not that bad."

The three of them headed back down to the street, hailed a cab, and took off for the airport.

32

The first thing Ali did when she got back to Georgia—after sleeping for almost twelve hours, of course—was start looking for a job.

She was willing to try any job that would pay enough to keep her in school, but it wasn't looking too good. So far she'd been rejected as a party clown, a military barber, a shoe shiner and a ticket taker at the movie theater.[23]

Finally she ended up at a café called the Greek Goddess with a resume specially doctored to make her look like an experienced waitress. She'd made it up at the student copy center that morning—listing several of the restaurants she and her friends had been to in Paris. She'd even given herself three years experience waitressing at Angelina on the rue de Rivoli.

Unfortunately, the Greek Goddess wasn't impressed. "So you've only worked in France?" the stuck-up woman in charge of hiring asked her.

□□□□□□□□□□□□□□□□□□□□□□□□□□□□□□
23 She'd asked if friends could get in free.

"That's right," Ali said.

"So I assume you speak French," the woman said.

"Uh, *oui*," Ali said. *"Je m'appelle Ali."*

"Great, you know your name. Very impressive," the woman said, looking down her nose at her. *"Voulez-vous un peu lait avec votre chocolat?"*

Huh? Ali thought, blanching. She'd recognized the word *chocolate*. "Um—*quatorze?*" she tried.

"Yeah, right. I'm in the graduate French program, Miss Sheppard, and you're shit out of luck," the woman said, slapping her fake resume back into her hand. "Why don't you try the Starbucks across campus?"

Ali left with her tail between her legs, feeling beaten down by life once again, until she was stopped by a strange man who had been sitting in the café eating spanakopita while she suffered through her pathetic interview.

"So you're looking for a job?" the man said. He took a cigar out of his pocket and put it, unlit, into his mouth. His teeth were kind of yellow and his hair was kind of nonexistent—just little tufts around his ears.

"Yes," Ali said, slightly suspiciously. She was extra careful with strange men after her experience with Rocco Lee.

"Well, I was very impressed with you in there," the guy said, wiping his hand on the front of his wrinkled Hawaiian shirt. "Let's just say I like the way you lie. I admire that in a bird. I need some assistance and I'm willing to give you a crack at it."

Bird? Crack at it? Who talked like that? "Who are you?" Ali asked.

"Milton Copley, private eye," the man said.

"You mean I'm going to be a spy?" Ali asked. She loved the idea. And what could be better than getting a job for lying well?

Milton laughed as much as you can laugh with a cigar in your mouth. He almost choked himself.

"More like a secretary to a spy," Milton said, handing her his card. "Ten bucks an hour. You can start tonight. I need someone in the office while I'm on stakeout."

Ali grinned. She had a job! A great job that didn't involve big polka-dotted shoes or touching people's hair or serving overpriced, undercooked Greek food.

"Thanks! I'll be there!" Ali said, checking out the address of his office.

Feeling suddenly lighter than air, Ali walked over to student services and signed up for free tutoring. Now that she had a job, she was going to get her grades back on track as well. Say hello to the new, responsible Ali!

33

While Ali was becoming responsible, Celeste was on her way to music humanities, a class she was beginning to dread with her entire soul. Every time she saw Professor McKean, she just relived her lie over and over again. Plus there was gross Carter Mann, who had never even called her again, taking up space in the back row.

As Celeste studiously kept her eyes straight ahead and away from Carter, a thought occurred to her. The guy really did seem to love Jib's pot. Very much. And Jib had plenty of it. *What if I sold him some?* Celeste wondered. It wouldn't technically be drug dealing, because all the proceeds would be going to charity— keeping Ali in school. Okay, okay, it was drug dealing, but desperate times called for desperate measures, as Sartre would say.

Celeste took a deep breath as she considered taking this step into a world of crime. Actually, ever since she had gotten back from Paris, she'd been seriously considering becoming a writer and maybe living in France for a few years after college. And if she was going to be a writer, she should have a lot of interesting experiences first. Like drug dealing.

She was so caught up in figuring out how to approach Carter and save Ali and turn it all into a best-selling novel, that she barely noticed class was over and practically everyone had already left the room. Celeste turned around in her seat and actually breathed a sigh of relief when she saw Carter was still there. She picked up her books and approached the back of the room.

"Hi, Carter," Celeste said, very flirtatiously. After all, this might one day be a scene in a novel.

"Hi, Celeste," Carter said, smiling at her. "You weren't in class on Friday."

"Oh, well, I went to Paris unexpectedly," she said, showing off just a little.

"Whoa, that's pretty cool," he said.

"Anyway, I really had a great time with you in the peach orchard—"

"Yeah! It was nice," Carter said. "That weed you had was amazing."

"For sure," Celeste said. "And it's hard to get such great-quality stuff."

"I know it is, believe me," Carter said. "I'd do anything to get my hands on some more of that."

"Really?" Celeste asked. "It's funny you should say that, because I might be able to get you some more, if you're interested, and if you don't mind paying top dollar for it in, um, bulk."

"No!" Carter said.

"Oh, uh, okay," Celeste replied, sort of crushed.

"I mean, no, I don't mind paying top dollar. And yes, I

would be very interested in buying as much as you can get me."

"That's great!" Celeste said, forgetting for a moment where she was. Boy, drug dealing was easy! "I'll get you the pot right away." That was when she realized that the few people who had stayed after class had fallen silent and were all staring at her.

"-atoes," she added, blushing. "Potatoes."

"Thanks," Carter said. "Just let me know when you get your hands on it."

He walked out the back door, and Celeste smiled sheepishly at the others. She was about to make a run for it when she was stopped by Eve, the girl from the Lesbian Alliance who always stared at her.

"I know what happened," Eve said, flicking her braid over her shoulder.

"Oh, it's not what you think," Celeste said. "It's potatoes. Uh . . . potato chips. These special chips Carter likes that I can get in New York." This was awful. Eve would probably turn her in to the dean and she would be expelled.

"No, I mean about Professor McKean kissing you after class. I saw it coming, you know."

"What!?" Celeste asked, mortified. What the hell was going on? How could Eve have seen something coming that never even happened?

"What he did was wrong. Forcing you to kiss him and threatening to fail you if you didn't comply with his sick request," Eve said.

"But—"

"I am very surprised that you have not filed a sexual

harassment charge against Professor McKean, and frankly, if you don't, I will in your name," Eve continued, starting to get all worked up. "He must be stopped. Who knows how many young PU women he's harassed? Perverts like him should not be teaching at our school."

"How did you find out about this?" Celeste asked, feeling nauseated. Was Eve one of the people Ali had bumped into at Dimers?

"It's all over campus, Celeste," Eve said with a look of disbelief at Celeste's ignorance.

All over campus? But *how*?

"No, Eve, you have it wrong," Celeste said, tears coming to her eyes. She was really starting to panic. "I lied. The whole thing is a lie."

"Celeste, it's very common for victims to protect their abusers," Eve said, putting her hand on Celeste's shoulder. "I mean, come on, why would anyone lie about something like that?"

Celeste didn't know what to say. She couldn't tell Eve about the AHUL because it was a total secret. And it probably wouldn't sound real, anyway.

"I don't know why I lied, but it's not Professor McKean's fault," Celeste cried.

"Celeste," Eve said, in a voice filled with pity. "I don't believe you. Professor McKean is a very bad man, and I'm going to help you to put an end to this."

"But—"

"You can count on me," Eve said. She turned on her heel and walked out, leaving Celeste feeling worse than she had ever felt in her life. Now she was really in deep.

34

Ali met with her tutor, Parker,[24] at the library for three intense hours. Minus just a few minutes here and there when Ali thought about how Parker was such a great tutor and how his name started with *P*, which was the next letter she needed, they actually studied. Really studied.

They got through five chapters of her French textbook, and Ali felt like she might have a chance at passing the next exam. And that was after just one session. If they met like this three times a week, she would definitely, possibly pass. If she had just done this from the beginning, she thought, she never would have gotten so behind.

"You know, I just got back from Paris," Ali said to Parker. She really liked hearing herself say that.

"You're kidding," he said. "Did you go to the Louvre? I've always wanted to go there."

"Of course," Ali lied. She didn't want to admit that not

24 She would have gotten a tutor a long time ago if she'd known they were this cute.

only was she failing French, she also hadn't bothered with the whole Louvre thing.

"What was it like to see the *Mona Lisa*?" he asked.

"Oh, it was amazing," Ali said. "She's huge, and she just kind of stares down at you."

"What?" Parker said. "Everyone has always told me they can't believe how small the painting is."

"Oh, yeah, it is small in *size*," Ali said. "But it's so intense that it feels huge."

Parker opened his mouth to ask something else, but considering Ali knew nothing else about the Louvre, she decided to kiss him instead. She grabbed both sides of his face and stopped his mouth with a nice, big, wet one. And why not? She had been so good with her studying, and she had shown restraint for hours. She deserved a little fun.

"What was that for?" Parker asked, smiling.

"For helping me," Ali said.

She felt fantastic. She went directly to French class from the library and totally impressed Monsieur Schwartz with tales of her impromptu trip to Paris. She even threw in a bit about her surprise at the small size of the *Mona Lisa* and Schwartz was so impressed, he gave her extra credit for going to the Louvre on her free time.

After class Ali floated back to the triple, feeling better than she had felt in weeks. She had a job and a tutor and some extra credit *and* she was officially up to *Q*.

But the moment she opened the door to her room, a wild-eyed Celeste greeted her.

"How does everybody know I kissed Professor McKean?" Celeste demanded. "Did those people at Dimers already know about it, or did you tell them?"

Ali had never seen her like this. "I don't know. Maybe I did mention it first," she said, feeling a lump form in her stomach. "Why? What happened?"

"That Lesbian Alliance girl, Eve, is filing a sexual harassment claim against Professor McKean because she found out that I kissed him!" Celeste said.

"Wait a minute, Eve with the braids and the overalls?" Ali asked.

"Yeah, that's her," Celeste said.

"She was at Dimers that day," Ali said, her stomach turning as she thought back. "Omigod! She's one of the girls I kissed before you guys said girls couldn't count!" she added. "You don't think she actually likes me and is using this thing with you to get back at me for the kiss-and-run, do you?"

"I don't know!" Celeste cried, hardly able to believe she was having this conversation. "All I know is I'm in serious trouble."

"I'm sorry," Ali said. "I might have blabbed to her that day. It was after the Rocco Lee thing and I was totally trashed. I'm really sorry, Celeste."

"What am I going to do?" Celeste cried. She wanted to tell Ali that the whole thing had been a lie, but she just couldn't do it. Besides, confessing wouldn't make matters any better. It wouldn't change anything. "How are we going to get this girl to back off? You have to help me, Ali."

"I will," Ali said. "I swear I'm going to figure out some

way to help you. Just give me a couple of days and I'll figure something out."

"Do you promise?" Celeste asked.

"I promise," Ali said. She handed Celeste a roll of skinny-ass French toilet paper to dry her eyes with.

35

Jodi stood outside Zack's dorm room, debating whether or not to knock. She felt as if she were going crazy. It was so weird to be back on campus and not see him. He didn't even know she had been all the way to Paris and back.[25] That thought made her feel unbelievably lonely.

But he was clearly over her. There hadn't been any messages from him on their answering machine or on the message board on their door.

So what the hell was she doing here, hovering in his hallway?

Jodi looked at the present she had secretly bought him in Paris, when she had sneaked away from the others for a few minutes. It was silly, really. It was a red T-shirt with a cow on it, wearing a beret and holding a baguette under its arm. For some reason she thought he might get a kick out of it. And it had made her happy to buy it, like he was really her boyfriend.

"Oh, what the hell," she said under her breath.

□□□□□□□□□□□□□□□□□□□□□□□□□□□

25 The postcard she'd written him in a weak moment remained safely unsent in her purse.

She stuffed the T-shirt back into its plastic bag and was about to loop the handles around his doorknob when it turned. The door opened, and she was standing face-to-face with Zack. Jodi's heart skipped a beat. He looked good—*very* good—in a plain black T-shirt and beat-up jeans.

"Hi, Jodi," he said.

"Hi."

"That's not some kind of doorknob bomb, is it?" he asked, pointing to the plastic bag.

"No, it's a cow T-shirt. I went to Paris, and I bought it for you." She handed it to him.

"Yeah, I heard you went to Paris," he said.

"You did? How?"

"I went looking for you, and that girl with the lazy eye who lives next door to you said you were in France," he explained.

"You came looking for me?" Jodi asked, feeling suddenly breathless.

"Yeah. I wanted to . . . you know." Zack paused and took a deep breath, looking at the ceiling. "Do you want to come in?"

Jodi smiled. Did she ever.

Zack stepped aside so that she could slip by him. One side of his room was decorated like it was going to be hosting some kind of Confederate rally. A huge Confederate flag took up one whole wall, and it was surrounded by Civil War posters and paraphernalia. The other side of the room had a neatly made bed with a plaid bedspread and a bunch of vintage rock posters—the Doors, the Clash, the Who. Jodi took a stab in the dark and sat down on the plaid bed.

"I'm guessing this is your side," she said, eyeing the other bed warily.

"Don't even get me started about him," Zack said, rubbing the back of his neck as he turned toward her.

"Anyway, Jodi, listen," he began. "I'm sorry about the way I treated you at the library that day. I just . . . I didn't know what to say."

"Yeah. Me neither," Jodi said honestly. She swallowed hard. Did he not know what to say to blow her off, or did he not know what to say to tell her he liked her?

He sat down slowly on the bed next to her. The springs whined in protest. "But now that I've had some time to think about it . . . whatever I said that night we . . . you know . . . hooked up, I don't think this friends thing is going to work."

Jodi's heart sank. "Oh," she said, pressing her damp palms into her jeans. "Okay." She managed to look him in the eye. He was only inches away. "Why not?"

"Because. Because I like you—a lot," he said. "I think you know that."

Jodi smiled. She wasn't about to tell him that until this moment, she had no idea.

"I like you, too," she said. "A lot."

Zack's smile was heart-melting. "Then I'm going to amend my earlier statement. I don't care how on the rebound you are. I'm going to kiss you now, and then . . . I'd like to go out with you sometime."

"Okay," Jodi said, already swimming in a sea of giddiness.

Zack reached out and cupped her face with his hands and

just as Jodi's eyes fluttered closed, he gave her the most incredible, soul-shaking kiss she'd ever experienced. Even better than that night in the library. Because now she knew he felt the same way and everything was perfect.

Except for one nagging detail.

What was she going to do about the AHUL?

36

The next week was one of the best weeks of Jodi's life.[26] She and Zack were totally happy together. They napped together, they ate together, they went to movies and even studied a little together. Zack even said the dreaded *T*-word[27]. Maybe he would come home with her to Long Island to meet her parents.

But there was a little sadness in all this. Jodi had actually talked about spending Thanksgiving with Ali and Celeste, and now she wanted to be with Zack, and only Zack, more than anything. She hadn't even told Ali and Celeste about Zack yet, and she wasn't sure why.

Maybe because she just couldn't admit that she wasn't one with them anymore. They'd all started the AHUL and become friends in the first place when they were commiserating about how badly guys sucked. They'd made a pact to complete the list and she didn't want to let them down.

Not that she was planning to. Even in the midst of all of

□□□□□□□□□□□□□□□□□□□□□□□□□□□□

26 If this were a movie, this paragraph would be a romantic montage sequence.

27 Thanksgiving.

her Zack-related happiness, Jodi decided that she had to finish the AHUL. She wasn't all that into it anymore, but it would be wrong to give up now. And as long as Zack didn't find out, it wasn't hurting anybody.

Anyway, she was already on *L*—almost halfway there. Maybe she'd just finish the whole thing off at her Intro to Film class next week.

Meanwhile Ali was studying up a storm with Parker and Celeste and was starting to get some of her papers and tests back. She was actually getting Cs and Bs, and when she earned one A in French, she felt stupefied. Or smartified. All that studying was actually paying off. She still had a lot of extra-credit work to do in order to catch up, but she was getting there.

And she loved her job working for Milton Copley, PI, in his office filled with old metal file cabinets that looked like something out of the 1930s—except for all of his minuscule cameras and see-in-the-dark stuff and fingerprint kits and surveillance binoculars and other newfangled gadgets. It was pretty much the coolest job in the whole world. He was only paying her for twenty hours a week, but she was staying longer and trying to convince him to give her a case.

"I tell you what, kid," Milton said. "I can't give you a case of your own, but if you bring one in, I'll help you crack it."

That's when it hit Ali that she did have a case! A very important case. Eve from the Lesbian Alliance. She needed to get some dirt on Eve. After all, it was probably her fault that Celeste's McKean secret got out in the first place.

She convinced Milton to let her use his camera with th—

telescopic lens. Then—and this was much harder—she tried to convince him to lend her his car.

"Oh, no," Milton said. "I'm not letting you take my Little Lassie."[28]

"Come on, dude, I won't hurt it," Ali pleaded.

"No way, *dude*," Milton said, smiling. He seemed to find the whole "dude" thing hilarious. "But I'll go with you."

"What should I wear?" Ali asked. She thought maybe she should find herself a London Fog raincoat and a fedora.

Milton looked at Ali in her ripped jeans and black V-necked T-shirt. "Wear something that makes you look like a dame," he said.

That evening Ali wore a skirt for Milton's sake. He picked her up in his Little Lassie, and they staked out Eve's car, which was parked in front of Abbey Hall. After about an hour, Eve showed up and got into her car alone. She pulled out of the parking lot, and they followed closely behind her.

After they had driven for about forty-five minutes, Eve pulled into the parking lot of a run-down motel. As Milton and Ali watched, Eve pulled off her boxy T-shirt to reveal a sexy tank underneath. Then she started wriggling around.

"What's she doing?" Milton asked.

"I have no idea," Ali replied.

Finally the wriggling stopped and Eve undid her braids, fluffed out her hair, and applied some lipstick, looking in the rearview mirror.

Lipstick! Ali took a picture with the long-distance camera. Since when was Eve a lipstick lesbian? At all the Lesbian

28 Milton's annoying name for his car.

Alliance meetings Ali had gone to earlier in the year, Eve had always been fresh-faced.

When Eve got out of her car, she looked like a different person. She was wearing the tiny tank top, a mini skirt, and *heels.* She took a quick look around and disappeared into the motel. What was going on?

"Should we follow her in there?" Ali asked.

"As a PI, always remember that your *pay* is in your *pay-tience,*" Milton said. "Just sit tight. Relax. Eat a doughnut. But don't get raspberry filling on my equipment." He handed her a waxy bag, but she was too excited to eat.

Then a cab pulled up and a guy with a cast on his leg, on crutches, got out and hobbled toward the motel.

"Oh my God," Ali said, taking about a million pictures. It was Buster Needham. Was it possible? Was Jodi's idiot ex-boyfriend having an affair with a pseudo-lesbian?

Sure enough, one hour later a cab pulled up and honked its horn. Eve and Buster came out of the motel, disheveled and giggly. Ali snapped some more shots, nailing Buster and Eve kissing goodnight. She even got a picture of Buster giving Eve one last grope. Yuck! Then Eve got into her car, Buster got into the cab, and they were gone.

Ali couldn't believe her eyes. She and Milton walked casually into the motel, gave the kid behind the desk five dollars, and got all the information they needed. It turned out Buster and Eve were regulars: they came three times a week, stayed an hour, and left.

Eve and Buster were doing it on a regular basis. Disgusting, but priceless. Ali couldn't wait to tell Celeste.

37

Armed with some eight-by-ten glossies, Celeste and Ali went to Eve's dorm room to confront her. As they walked up to her door, they heard a familiar voice on the other side.

"If you're so conflicted, then what was all that screaming and moaning about last night?" Buster's voice asked in a teasing tone.

Celeste froze. He was unbelievable.

"I don't know," Eve's voice replied. "Why do you have to be so damn good in bed? I mean, the way you make me feel—"

"Yeah, baby," Buster said, totally self-satisfied.

"I hate you," Eve said. "Because of you I'm turning my back on everything I believe in."

"Yeah? Believe in this," Buster said.

"Oh, Buster," Eve half moaned.

Celeste's jaw dropped open, and she looked at Ali. She didn't even want to *know* what was going on behind those walls. Ali, however, lifted her hand and rapped loudly on the door. There was a crash inside, and Celeste had to slap her hand over her mouth to keep from laughing.

Eve and Buster both came to the door—fully clothed, thank God—and Buster's face went white when he saw them.

"I gotta go," he said to Eve, and hobbled quickly off.

Eve pushed one messy braid behind her ear and opened the door wider. The room was wallpapered with lesbianesque posters, including a big sign over her bed that said *Embrace Your Homosexuality*.

Yeah, right, Ali thought. There was broken red glass all over the floor that looked like it had formerly made up a bong. Buster must have whacked it when he'd jumped off her moments ago.

"Celeste, I'm so glad you're here," Eve said, ignoring the fact that she'd just been caught with a hunk of oversexed man in her room. "I'm glad you've finally come to me for help. I know it's hard to talk about what that animal did to you, but I'm here for you."

"Actually," Celeste said, "we're here to ask you not to go to the administration with that rumor about the kiss."

"I'm sorry, Celeste, but I have to," Eve said firmly. "Fighting sexual harassment is one of the things the Lesbian Alliance feels very strongly about, and I hope to run for president of the Alliance next year."

Celeste and Ali exchanged a glance.

"Don't you, um, have to be a lesbian to be in the Lesbian Alliance?" Ali asked.

"Of course," Eve said.

"Oh, so then you probably wouldn't want your Lesbian Alliance pals finding out about Buster," Ali said.

"What are you talking about?" Eve asked, seeming totally calm. "We were just studying."

"Whatever. We know that you fuck Buster three times a week at the crappy motel off campus," Ali shot back. "Tell me, does he pay the hourly rate, or do you? I mean, considering the way he makes you *feel* . . ."

Eve went ashen, but she wasn't ready to give up. "I have no idea what you're talking about!" she insisted.

"Maybe these pictures will remind you," Celeste said. She pulled out Ali's quite impressive photos and dropped them on Eve's bed, where they fanned out in a colorful arc.

Hand shaking, Eve picked up the top photo—the one where she was leaning back and laughing while Buster grabbed her breast.

"Uh . . . he was . . . I mean, I—"

"Save it," Ali said. "We know about the screaming and moaning."

Eve's arm dropped to her side. "What do you want?" she asked, sounding defeated.

Celeste's heart leapt happily. Ali had saved her.

"We want you to drop this whole Professor McKean thing," Ali said.

"You have to tell people *you* made it up," Celeste added.

"And if you ever breathe another word about it, I will personally hand deliver these pictures to everyone you know," Ali said.

"Okay, okay," Eve said, practically in tears. "Consider the matter dropped."

"And really, Eve—Buster? If you wanted to come over to

our side you could have picked someone a little classier than him," Celeste said.

The moment Eve's door closed behind them, Ali and Celeste hugged giddily and headed for home. They practically skipped up the steps to their floor. But when Celeste opened the door, she stepped on an envelope that had been slid underneath. It had Ali's name on it. And it was from the bursar. Ali opened the envelope gingerly, and her smile evaporated.

"What's wrong?" Celeste asked.

Ali looked up with a stricken expression. "My tuition is late," she said. "I have to pay the whole thing in ten days— or I'm out."

38

The following morning, Celeste bolted out of bed the moment there was a knock on the door of the triple. Jodi had slept out again, though Celeste had no idea where, but Ali was still asleep. Celeste flew to the door before they could knock again. She wasn't at all surprised to see the UPS guy standing there. Right on time.

"Shhh! My roommate's sleeping," Celeste said, before he could speak.

He nodded his understanding, and Celeste signed for the package. Good old Jib. She placed the box on her bed, slipped into a pair of jeans and a sweatshirt, and put her curly hair up in a ponytail. Then she grabbed the box and slipped out so quietly, Ali never even stirred.

Out in the deserted lounge, Celeste opened the box to find more pot, more cookies, and another note from Jib saying that he and her mother were so glad she was experiencing new things. Little did her father know that this pot wasn't for her. She felt a little guilty letting her parents think she'd finally come around to their stoned way of life, but it was all for a good cause.

Celeste tucked the box under her arm and glanced at the door to room 213 as she walked toward the stairwell. Ali had no idea what she was about to do, and that was how Celeste wanted it. She'd tell her later, after the deed was done. If she told her now, Ali would definitely try to stop her.

Heart pounding, Celeste speed-walked to the meeting place she'd set up with Carter on the phone the night before—the perpetually deserted sixth floor of the library stacks. All the old magazines and *Facts On File* were housed up there, and the place was like a ghost town, especially early in the morning. Carter was sitting at the last carrel at the very back of the room.

"You got the stuff?" he asked from behind a pair of dark sunglasses. What was this? A bad cop spoof?

"Of course I got it," Celeste said. "Would I be here if I didn't?"

She handed him the box, and his eyes widened. "I don't know if I can afford all this stuff."

Celeste started to sweat. Was that a footstep she heard? "You said top dollar," she hissed.

"Well, how much do you want?" he asked.

She'd been afraid of this. Celeste had no idea how much good pot went for. All she knew was that Ali needed a few thousand dollars.

"I'll give you a grand for the lot," Carter said before she had thought up a price. But he blinked when he said it. That meant he was trying to get one over on her. Thank God for Psych 101!

"What are you, kidding?" Celeste said. "It's worth twice that much." Maybe.

"All right," Carter said. "Then I'll take half of it, for a grand."

Celeste sighed. Well, a thousand dollars was better than nothing. Carter popped open the tin of cookies and inhaled their buttery scent, then smiled happily.

"It's fifty bucks extra if you want the snacks," Celeste said before she even realized she'd thought it.

"Deal," Carter said. He handed Celeste a roll of money, then took an extra fifty out of his wallet and handed that over as well. Then he took one of the two baggies of pot out of the box and handed it to her. Celeste quickly slipped it into the pocket on the front of her sweatshirt.

"I'll go down first," Carter said, gathering up the box and looking around, already seeming paranoid. "Thanks, kid."

He stood up and gave her a kiss on the forehead. Celeste laughed as he walked away. That kiss would never have gotten her anywhere on the AHUL, even if she hadn't already gotten her C. But at least Carter was good for something. She looked at the wad of cash in her hand and sighed. Ali was a little bit closer to her goal.

39

That afternoon Ali went to Dimers and ordered a beer. It was pretty much the only thing in the world she could afford. She hadn't seen Celeste or Jodi all day, and she was feeling seriously depressed. She had to figure out a way to pay for her semester. Unfortunately, three skanky beers and thirty cents later, she still had no solution.

Bored and lonely, Ali looked around the room for a cute guy to kiss. The AHUL was sort of addictive that way. If she had to leave PU, she might as well go out with a bang, win the contest, and collect her prize—her friends taking her out for a great night on the town.

She looked at the guy sitting next to her, who seemed to be absorbed in a book. He had sandy blond hair and was wearing a surfer tee with a string of tiny shells hung around his neck. She glanced over his shoulder to see what he was so interested in. He was reading a seriously tattered copy of *The Old Man and the Sea.*

Huh. Ali was down with Hemingway. This guy was a great

candidate, no matter what his name was. Her lips were practically tingling with anticipation.

"Hi," she said.

He looked up, took a sip of his beer, and smiled. "Hey," he replied.

"So, Hemingway huh?" Ali said. "I loved *For Whom the Bell Tolls.*"

"Yeah?" he said, folding the book closed. "This is the only book of his I've ever read."

"And it looks like you've read it a *lot,*" Ali said. "I'm more into his romances. They're so tragic."

"Are you in a tragic mood?" he asked, taking another sip and eyeing her with a flirtatious look.

"Maybe I'm in a romantic mood," she said.

Ali started to lean in, but Hemingway guy looked away. "I don't think I've ever read anything that could be considered a romance."

"Figures. You're a guy," Ali said with a shrug. She felt a bit deflated at being rejected, but when he laughed, a little chill skittered over Ali's skin. He had a sexy laugh.

"You know, I was just about to kiss you," she said bluntly.

"I thought you might be," he said.

"And you didn't want to?" Ali asked, hurt.

"It's not that I didn't want to," he said, leaning his elbow on the bar so he could turn toward her. "It just seems to me that something's bothering you and what you really need is to have someone listen to you."

Ali frowned in thought. Maybe this was exactly what she

needed—an outsider's opinion. And here he was, ready and willing. Why not? She'd had four beers now. She was ready to spill.

"Okay, it all started with this check I got from my dad," Ali began. She went through the whole embarrassing story from Rocco Lee to Paris and back to Pollard. The whole time, she was talking, Hemingway watched her closely, nodding and grimacing at all the right places.

"So what do you think?" she asked when she was done.

"I think it's an amazing story," he said. "And even if you do have to leave Pollard, I'm guessing you're still going to have a lot of adventures. Whatever else happens, your life will never be boring. But if I were you, I'd try to work something out with the bursar's office before you give up."

Ali smiled. Not that he had solved her problem, but it was nice just to *talk* to him. How long had it been since she'd talked to a guy without trying to figure out a way to kiss him? "Thank you," she said.

"Anytime," he said. Finishing off the last of his beer, he stood up. "Well, I have to get to class. See you around."

"See you." Ali sat back on her stool, feeling thoughtful.

Wow. Boys really could be good for something other than kissing.

40

That night, Ali walked over to the student activity center with a note from Celeste and Jodi tucked in her pocket. It said to meet them there at eight o'clock and that they had a surprise for her. Ali had no idea what was going on, but she was glad she was going to see her two roomies. They'd barely been in the same room together for more than five minutes since they got back from Paris.

Ali spotted them waiting outside the brightly lit, sprawling building and waved.

"Surprise!" Celeste and Jodi shouted as Ali approached. Celeste thrust an envelope into Ali's hands. A very thick envelope.

"What is this?" she asked as she opened it. She gasped when she saw the stack of bills inside. "How much is here?"

"One thousand, two hundred and fifty-six dollars," Jodi and Celeste announced at the same time. A couple of guys stopped and eyed them on the way into the center, and Celeste realized they should keep their voices down.

"Jodi put in the two hundred six," Celeste whispered, stepping closer to Ali. "It's money she was saving for new sheets and stuff."

"And you're not going to believe what Celeste did for the one-thousand fifty," Jodi exclaimed.

"Slut," Ali joked, looking at Celeste out of the corner of her eye.

"I'm not a hooker!" Celeste protested, coloring. Then she giggled. "But I am a drug dealer."

"What?" Ali said, almost dropping the money.

"I sold some of Jib's pot to geriatric Carter," Celeste said proudly.

"I can't believe you!" Ali said with a grin. "Jodi, we're really corrupting her."

"Well, we have one more vice to tackle," Jodi said, looking at the student activity center. "Gambling."

Celeste and Jodi ushered Ali into the main room of the activities center. The place was jumping. A huge banner that read *Casino Night!* was draped across the back wall and there were tables placed all over the room. Students were playing blackjack, poker, roulette, craps and a ton of other whirring, blinking, noisy games. Hundreds of people were milling around laughing and whooping as they won big hands.

"We figure you have another five hundred to make," Jodi said with a nod. "Might as well go for it."

"You guys, this is so cool," Ali said, "but I can't take your money. You earned it."

"*You* took *us* to Paris," Celeste said, raising her hands as Ali tried to hand her the envelope. "That money is yours."

"Now let's go play!" Jodi said, slipping out of her denim

jacket. She tied it around her waist and dragged Ali toward the roulette wheel. It seemed like the safest bet.

With Celeste and Jodi on either side of her, Ali decided to bet ten dollars on each roll of the wheel—one dollar on each of ten numbers. The first few rounds she lost it all, and she started to feel ill. Thirty bucks down the drain! Then, when she put a dollar down on 13 in honor of their room, Celeste and Jodi each put a dollar on as well.

The guy running the roulette table—a chubby guy about their age—spun the wheel and it came up 13! Ali, Jodi, and Celeste cheered and hugged, then cheered and hugged again when they found out how much their three-dollar bet paid out—$120! They'd be up to $500 in no time!

"You guys, I have to go to the bathroom," Jodi told them as they placed another ten dollars on the board. "I'll be right back."

She jogged across the room, but when she came around the corner, the line for the bathroom was snaking out into the lobby. She sighed and joined the hordes of bladder-challenged girls.[29] Leaning against the wall, Jodi found herself wishing Zack had come tonight. She'd left him a message this morning, telling him she'd be here, and he'd left her a message back telling her he had to work. Too bad. He would have gotten a kick out of a bunch of people throwing their hard-earned money away. Then again, she would have had to hang out with him in stealth mode to keep Celeste and Ali from finding out about their relationship.

□□□□□□□□□□□□□□□□□□□□□□□□□□□□
29 There was, of course, no line for the men's room.

The door to the men's room opened, and a tall, slim guy with shaggy brown hair and green eyes walked out. He looked at her, then did a double take as if he knew her. Unfortunately, Jodi had never seen the guy before in her life.

"Hey! You and your friends just cleaned up at the roulette wheel, right?" he asked.

"Yeah, I guess so," Jodi replied.

"What's your secret?" he asked, standing next to her as the line inched forward.

"Playing our lucky numbers, I guess," she said. He laughed, and Jodi looked him up and down. He was kind of cute, in a gawky sort of way. Plus he had a cool red-and-yellow guitar tattoo that took him up a couple of notches on the kissable scale. Could she possibly be so lucky as to have found an *L*? "What's your name?" she asked. "You look like a Larry to me."

"Not quite," he said with a funny smile. "But you got the initial right. I'm Lucas." He extended his hand to shake.

Unreal! Jodi shook his hand, then pulled him toward her, standing on her toes to kiss him. All she could think as he was fumbling to respond was, *I've got my L!* One more step closer to freedom! One more step closer to being free to date Zack! And when she got to *Z*, was she ever going to give Zack the kiss of a lifetime!

The moment Jodi pulled away from Lucas, she saw someone staring at them from the corner of her eye. She looked over to find Zack standing next to the men's-room door, a stricken expression on his face.

Oh God. This was not happening.

"Hey, I—" Lucas began.

"I have to go," she managed, waving him away. She took a shaky step out of line toward Zack. He took a step back. "What're you . . . what're you doing here?" Jodi asked, knowing it was so not the issue.

"I got the night off to surprise you," Zack said, stuffing his hands into the front pockets of his jeans. "Who was that you were kissing?"

Jodi opened her mouth to explain, but Zack cut her off. "Actually, forget I asked," he went on, shaking his head slightly. "I already know I can't trust you, and I guess that's all I need to know."

He turned and stalked through the lobby, then disappeared through the front door. Tears sprang to Jodi's eyes. Her first instinct was to chase him, but what would be the point? How could she possibly explain her reasons for kissing Lucas?

She turned around, blurry eyed, and rushed back to the casino room. She didn't even notice that Lucas had disappeared as well.

41

"Three! We have a winner!" the fat croupier at the roulette table announced.

Ali's mouth dropped open. "Did he just say three?" she asked, looking at Celeste.

"Why? How much did you have on three?" Celeste asked, peeking over the side of the table.

"Ten dollars!" Ali said, stunned. She quickly did the math in her head. "That's . . . that's . . . "

"Four hundred to the lucky lady!" the fat guy announced, handing over the chips.

Ali took them, and she and Celeste started jumping up and down, clutching each other's arms.

"We did it!" Celeste shouted. "You have enough to pay your tuition!"

Still grasping the chips, Ali threw her arms around Celeste and hugged her. She glanced at the croupier. "Dude, how can I thank you?"

"What's your name?" Celeste asked with a sly smile.

"Me?" The croupier looked surprised. "Quincy."

Ali and Celeste stared at each other. "Dude, this is *spooky*," Ali whispered. Stepping forward, she planted a long, heartfelt kiss on Quincy's lips.

She stepped back, grinning. "*Q*," she announced. But her smile faded as she saw Jodi rushing toward them through the crowd. Tears were streaming down her cheeks.

"Jodi? What's wrong?" Ali said, releasing Celeste.

Celeste turned around, took one look at Jodi, and pulled her friends toward the wall for some privacy.

"Can we get out of here?" Jodi asked.

"Absolutely," Ali said, quickly pocketing her winnings. She would have left even if she'd *lost* $520. Jodi obviously needed to powwow. They cashed in their chips and headed outside, then slumped onto the first bench they found.

"What's going on?" Celeste asked, slipping her arm around Jodi's shoulders.

"I really messed up, you guys," Jodi said. She took in a shaky breath and looked at them. "I've been seeing Zack behind your backs."

"Zack from the dining hall?" Ali asked, confused. "Why?"

"Because! He's so cute and perfect and smart and—"

"Not why are you seeing him," Ali interrupted. "Why are you seeing him behind our backs? I think it's great. Zack is a hottie. And you deserve the best after the bust that was Buster."

"Thanks," Jodi said. But then she convulsed with sobs all over again.

"That's not all, is it?" Celeste asked.

"No!" Jodi cried. "He just caught me kissing some guitar-tattoo-sporting guy named Lucas. He said he couldn't trust me, and he walked out. All so I could get my *L*!"

"Come on," Ali said. "He'll get over it."

"I don't know. You didn't see the look on his face," Jodi replied with a sniffle. "He looked heartbroken."

Celeste squirmed on the bench. This was unbelievable. Jodi had found this great guy, and because of the Alphabetical Hookup List, she'd lost him. Just like that.

And—wait a second. A guitar tattoo?

"Hey, Jodi, what did Lucas look like?" Celeste asked.

"He was kind of tall with scruffy dark hair," Jodi said with a shrug. "Green eyes, I think. I don't know. He was cute, he had a red-and-yellow tattoo on his arm, that's about it."

"I don't believe this," Celeste said, fuming. "*I* kissed a tall, scruffy-haired guy with a guitar tattoo, but he told me his name was David!"

"What?" Jodi asked, horrified. "Why didn't he give me his real name?"

Ali frowned. Hadn't a guy with a red-and-yellow guitar tattoo come on to her at Dimers? But it couldn't be the same guy, right? His name was Mark.

"I don't know," Celeste answered. "What an asshole."

She leaned back into the bench and stared out across campus. She couldn't take this anymore. In a matter of a few weeks she'd become a lying, drunken-sex-having adulterer, and for what? So that Jodi could lose the potential love of her life? So that they could both get used by some coed-kissing freak?

Celeste looked at Ali's bewildered face and Jodi's tear-swollen one and made a resolution right then and there.

She was done with the Alphabetical Hookup List. For good.

More on the way...

The Alphabetical Hookup List

An all-new series

A–J
K-Q
R-Z

Three sizzling new titles
Coming soon from
PHOEBE McPHEE
and MTV Books

www.mtv.com

www.alloy.com

Like this is the only one...

Floating
Robin Troy

The Perks of Being a Wallflower
Stephen Chbosky

The Fuck-up
Arthur Nersesian

Dreamworld
Jane Goldman

Fake Liar Cheat
Tod Goldberg

Pieces
edited by Stephen Chbosky

Dogrun
Arthur Nersesian

Brave New Girl
Louisa Luna

The Foreigner
Meg Castaldo

Tunnel Vision
Keith Lowe

Number Six Fumbles
Rachel Solar-Tuttle

Crooked
Louisa Luna

Don't Sleep with Your Drummer
Jen Sincero

More from the young, the hip,
and the up-and-coming.
Brought to you by MTV Books.

POCKET
BOOKS

Printed in the United States
By Bookmasters